CW01212761

THE HUMAN COMEDY
AND OTHER SHORT NOVELS

Copyright © BiblioBazaar, LLC

BiblioBazaar Reproduction Series: Our goal at BiblioBazaar is to help readers, educators and researchers by bringing back in print hard-to-find original publications at a reasonable price and, at the same time, preserve the legacy of literary history. The following book represents an authentic reproduction of the text as printed by the original publisher and may contain prior copyright references. While we have attempted to accurately maintain the integrity of the original work(s), from time to time there are problems with the original book scan that may result in minor errors in the reproduction, including imperfections such as missing and blurred pages, poor pictures, markings and other reproduction issues beyond our control. Because this work is culturally important, we have made it available as a part of our commitment to protecting, preserving and promoting the world's literature.

All of our books are in the "public domain" and many are derived from Open Source projects dedicated to digitizing historic literature. We believe that when we undertake the difficult task of re-creating them as attractive, readable and affordable books, we further the mutual goal of sharing these works with a larger audience. A portion of Bibliobazaar profits go back to Open Source projects in the form of a donation to the groups that do this important work around the world. If you would like to make a donation to these worthy Open Source projects, or would just like to get more information about these important initiatives, please visit www.bibliobazaar.com/opensource.

HONORE DE BALZAC

THE HUMAN COMEDY
AND OTHER SHORT NOVELS

BIBLIOBAZAAR

THE HUMAN COMEDY
AND OTHER SHORT NOVELS

CONTENTS

THE HUMAN COMEDY:
    INTRODUCTIONS AND APPENDIX 9

MELMOTH RECONCILED 63

UNCONSCIOUS COMEDIANS 111

THE HUMAN COMEDY:

INTRODUCTIONS AND APPENDIX

HONORE DE BALZAC

"Sans genie, je suis flambe!"

Volumes, almost libraries, have been written about Balzac; and perhaps of very few writers, putting aside the three or four greatest of all, is it so difficult to select one or a few short phrases which will in any way denote them, much more sum them up. Yet the five words quoted above, which come from an early letter to his sister when as yet he had not "found his way," characterize him, I think, better than at least some of the volumes I have read about him, and supply, when they are properly understood, the most valuable of all keys and companions for his comprehension.

"If I have not genius, it is all up with me!" A very matter-of-fact person may say: "Why! there is nothing wonderful in this. Everybody knows what genius is wanted to make a name in literature, and most people think they have it." But this would be a little short-sighted, and only excusable because of the way in which the word "genius" is too commonly bandied about. As a matter of fact, there is not so very much genius in the world; and a great deal of more than fair performance is attainable and attained by more or less decent allowances or exhibitions of talent. In prose, more especially, it is possible to gain a very high place, and to deserve it, without any genius at all: though it is difficult, if not impossible, to do so in verse. But what Balzac felt (whether he was conscious in detail of the feeling or not) when he used these words to his sister Laure, what his critical readers must feel when they have read only a very little of his work, what they must feel still more strongly when they have read that work as a whole—is that for him there is no such door of escape and no such compromise. He had the choice, by his nature, his aims, his capacities, of being a genius or nothing. He had no little gifts, and he was even destitute of some of the separate and indivisible great ones. In mere writing, mere style, he was not supreme; one seldom or never derives from anything of his the merely artistic satisfaction given by perfect prose. His humor, except of the grim and gigantic kind, was not remarkable; his wit, for a Frenchman, curiously thin and small. The minor felicities of the literature generally were denied to him. *Sans genie, il etait flambe; flambe* as he seemed to be, and very reasonably seemed, to his friends when as yet the genius had not come to him, and when he was desperately striving to discover where his genius lay in those wonderous works which "Lord R'Hoone," and "Horace de Saint Aubin," and others obligingly fathered for him.

It must be the business of these introductions to give what assistance they may to discover where it did lie; it is only necessary, before taking up the task in the regular biographical and critical way of the introductory cicerone, to make two negative observations. It did not lie, as some have apparently thought, in the conception, or the outlining, or the filling up of such a scheme as the *Comedie Humaine*. In the first place, the work of every great writer, of the creative kind, including that of Dante himself, is a *comedie humaine*. All humanity is latent in every human being; and the great writers are merely those who call most of it out of latency and put it actually on the stage. And, as students of Balzac know, the scheme and adjustment of his comedy varied so remarkably as time went on that it can hardly be said to have, even in its latest form (which would pretty certainly have been altered again), a distinct and definite character. Its so-called scenes are even in the mass by no means exhaustive, and are, as they stand, a very "cross," division of life: nor are they peopled by anything like an exhaustive selection of personages. Nor again is Balzac's genius by any means a mere vindication of the famous definition of that quality as an infinite capacity of taking pains. That Balzac had that capacity—had it in a degree probably unequaled even by the dullest plodders on record—is very well known, is one of the best known things about him. But he showed it for nearly ten years before the genius came, and though no doubt it helped him when genius had come, the two things are in his case, as in most, pretty sufficiently distinct. What the genius itself was I must do my best to indicate hereafter, always beseeching the reader to remember that all genius is in its essence and quiddity indefinable. You can no more get close to it than you can get close to the rainbow, and your most scientific explanation of it will always leave as much of the heart of the fact unexplained as the scientific explanation of the rainbow leaves of that.

Honore de Balzac was born at Tours on the 16th of May, 1799, in the same year which saw the birth of Heine, and which therefore had the honor of producing perhaps the most characteristic writers of the nineteenth century in prose and verse respectively. The family was a respectable one, though its right to the particle which Balzac always carefully assumed, subscribing himself *"de Balzac,"* was contested. And there appears to be no proof of their connection with Jean Guez de Balzac, the founder, as some will have him, of modern French prose, and the contemporary and fellow-reformer of Malherbe. (Indeed, as the novelist pointed out with sufficient pertinence, his earlier namesake had no hereditary right to the name at all, and merely took it from some property.) Balzac's father, who, as the *zac* pretty surely indicates, was a southerner and a native of Languedoc, was fifty-three years old at the birth of his son, whose Christian name was selected on the ordinary principle of accepting that of the saint on whose day he was born. Balzac the elder had been a barrister before the Revolution, but under it he obtained a post in the commissariat, and rose to be head of that department for a military division. His wife, who was much younger than himself and who survived her son, is said to have possessed both beauty and fortune, and was evidently endowed with the business faculties so common among Frenchwomen. When Honore was born, the family had not long been established at Tours, where Balzac the elder (besides his duties) had a house and some land; and this town continued to be their headquarters till the novelist, who was the eldest of the family, was about sixteen. He had two sisters (of whom the elder, Laure, afterwards Madame Surville, was his first confidante and his only authoritative biographer) and a younger brother, who seems to have been, if not a scapegrace, rather a burden to his friends, and who later went abroad.

The eldest boy was, in spite of Rousseau, put out to nurse, and at seven years old was sent to the Oratorian grammar-school at Vendome, where he stayed another seven years, going through, according to his own account, the future experiences and performances of Louis Lambert, but making no reputation for himself in the ordinary school course. If, however, he would not work in his teacher's way, he overworked himself in his own by devouring books; and was sent home at fourteen in such a state of health that his grandmother (who after the French fashion, was living with her daughter and son-in-law), ejaculated: *"Voila donc comme le college nous renvoie les jolis enfants que nous lui envoyons!"* It would seem indeed that, after making all due allowance for grandmotherly and sisterly partiality, Balzac was actually a very good-looking boy and young man, though the portraits of him in later life may not satisfy the more romantic expectations of his admirers. He must have had at all times eyes full of character, perhaps the only feature that never fails in men of intellectual eminence; but he certainly does not seem to have been in his manhood either exactly handsome or exactly "distinguished-looking." But the portraits of the middle of the century are, as a rule, rather wanting in this characteristic when compared with those of its first and last periods; and I cannot think of many that quite come up to one's expectations.

For a short time he was left pretty much to himself, and recovered rapidly. But late in 1814 a change of official duties removed the Balzacs to Paris, and when they had established themselves in the famous old *bourgeois* quarter of the Marais, Honore was sent to divers private tutors or private schools till he had "finished his classes" in 1816 at the age of seventeen and a half. Then he attended lectures at the Sorbonne where Villemain, Guizot, and Cousin were lecturing, and heard them, as his sister tells us, enthusiastically, though there are probably no three writers of any considerable repute in the history of French literature who stand further apart from Balzac. For all three made and kept their fame by spirited and agreeable generalizations and expatiations, as different as possible from the savage labor of observation on the one hand and the gigantic developments of imagination on the other, which were to compose Balzac's appeal. His father destined him for the law; and for three years more he dutifully attended the offices of an attorney and a notary, besides going through the necessary lectures and examinations. All these trials he seems to have passed, if not brilliantly, yet sufficiently.

And then came the inevitable crisis, which was of an unusually severe nature. A notary, who was a friend of the elder Balzac's and owed him some gratitude offered not merely to take Honore into his office, but to allow him to succeed to his business, which was a very good one, in a few years on very favorable terms. Most fathers, and nearly all French fathers, would have jumped at this; and it so happened that about the same time M. de Balzac was undergoing that unpleasant process of compulsory retirement which his son has described in one of the best passages of the *Oeuvres de Jeunesse*, the opening scene of *Argow le Pirate*. It does not appear that Honore had revolted during his probation—

indeed he is said, and we can easily believe it from his books, to have acquired a very solid knowledge of law, especially in bankruptcy matters, of which he was himself to have a very close shave in future. A solicitor, indeed, told Laure de Balzac that he found *Cesar Birotteau* a kind of *Balzac on Bankruptcy*; but this may have been only the solicitor's fun.

It was no part of Honore's intentions to use this knowledge—however content he had been to acquire it—in the least interesting, if nearly the most profitable, of the branches of the legal profession; and he protested eloquently, and not unsuccessfully, that he would be a man of letters and nothing else. Not unsuccessfully; but at the same time with distinctly qualified success. He was not turned out of doors; nor were the supplies, as in Quinet's case only a few months later, absolutely withheld even for a short time. But his mother (who seems to have been less placable than her husband) thought that cutting them down to the lowest point might have some effect. So, as the family at this time (April 1819) left Paris for a house some twenty miles out of it, she established her eldest son in a garret furnished in the most Spartan fashion, with a starvation allowance and an old woman to look after him. He did not literally stay in this garret for the ten years of his astonishing and unparalleled probation; but without too much metaphor it may be said to have been his Wilderness, and his Wanderings in it to have lasted for that very considerable time.

We know, in detail, very little of him during the period. For the first years, between 1819 and 1822, we have a good number of letters to Laure; between 1822 and 1829, when he first made his mark, very few. He began, of course, with verse, for which he never had the slightest vocation, and, almost equally of course, with a tragedy. But by degrees and apparently pretty soon, he slipped into what was his vocation, and like some, though not very many, great writers, at first did little better in it than if it had not been his vocation at all. The singular tentatives which, after being allowed for a time a sort of outhouse in the structure of the *Comedie Humaine*, were excluded from the octavo *Edition Definitive* five-and-twenty years ago, have never been the object of that exhaustive bibliographical and critical attention which has been bestowed on those which follow them. They were not absolutely unproductive—we hear of sixty, eighty, a hundred pounds being paid for them, though whether this was the amount of Balzac's always sanguine expectations, or hard cash actually handed over, we cannot say. They were very numerous, though the reprints spoken of above never extended to more than ten. Even these have never been widely read. The only person I ever knew till I began this present task who had read them through was the friend whom all his friends are now lamenting and are not likely soon to cease to lament, Mr. Louis Stevenson; and when I once asked him whether, on his honor and conscience, he could recommend me to brace myself to the same effort, he said that on his honor and conscience he must most earnestly dissuade me. I gather, though I am not sure, that Mr. Wedmore, the latest writer in English on Balzac at any length, had not read them through when he wrote.

Now I have, and a most curious study they are. Indeed I am not sorry, as Mr. Wedmore thinks one would be. They are curiously, interestingly, almost enthrallingly bad. Couched for the most part in a kind of Radcliffian or Monk-Lewisian vein—perhaps studied more directly from Maturin (of whom Balzac was a great admirer) than from either—they often begin with and sometimes contain at intervals passages not unlike the Balzac that we know. The attractive title of *Jane la Pale* (it was originally called, with a still more Early Romantic avidity for *baroque* titles, *Wann-Chlore*) has caused it, I believe, to be more commonly read than any other. It deals with a disguised duke, a villainous Italian, bigamy, a surprising offer of the angelic first wife to submit to a sort of double arrangement, the death of the second wife and first love, and a great many other things. *Argow le Pirate* opens quite decently and in order with that story of the *employe* which Balzac was to rehandle so often, but drops suddenly into brigands stopping diligences, the marriage of the heroine Annette with a retired pirate marquis of vast wealth, the trial of the latter for murdering another marquis with a poisoned fish-bone scarf-pin, his execution, the sanguinary reprisals by his redoubtable lieutenant, and a finale of blunderbusses, fire, devoted peasant girl with *retrousse* nose, and almost every possible *tremblement*.

In strictness mention of this should have been preceded by mention of *Le Vicaire des Ardennes*, which is a sort of first part of *Argow le Pirate*, and not only gives an account of his crimes, early history, and manners (which seem to have been a little robustious for such a mild-mannered man as Annette's husband), but tells a thrilling tale of the loves of the *vicaire* himself and a young woman, which loves are crossed, first by the belief that they are brother and sister, and secondly by the *vicaire* having taken orders under this delusion. *La Derniere Fee* is the queerest possible cross between an actual fairy story *a la* Nordier and a history of the fantastic and inconstant loves of a great English lady, the Duchess of "Sommerset" (a piece of actual *scandalum magnatum* nearly as bad as Balzac's cool use in his acknowledged work of the title "Lord Dudley"). This book begins so well that one expects it to go on better; but the inevitable defects in craftsmanship show themselves before long. *Le Centenaire* connects itself with Balzac's almost lifelong hankering after the *recherche de l'absolu* in one form or another, for the hero is a wicked old person who every now and then refreshes his hold on life by immolating a virgin under a copper-bell. It is one of the most extravagant and "Monk-Lewisy" of the whole. *L'Excommunié*, *L'Israelite*, and *L'Heritiere de Birague* are mediaeval or fifteenth century tales of the most luxuriant kind, *L'Excommunié* being the best, *L'Israelite* the most preposterous, and *L'Heritiere de Birague* the dullest. But it is not nearly so dull as *Dom Gigadus* and *Jean Louis*, the former of which deals with the end of the seventeenth century and the latter with the end of the eighteenth. These are both as nearly unreadable as anything can be. One interesting thing, however, should be noted in much of this early work: the affectionate clinging of the author to the scenery of Touraine, which sometimes inspires him with his least bad passages.

It is generally agreed that these singular *Oeuvres de Jeunesse* were of service to Balzac as exercise, and no doubt they were so; but I think something may be said on the other side. They must have done a little, if not much, to lead him into and confirm him in those defects of style and form which distinguish him so remarkably from most writers of his rank. It very seldom happens when a very young man writes very much, be it book-writing or journalism, without censure and without "editing," that he does not at the same time get into loose and slipshod habits. And I think we may set down to this peculiar form of apprenticeship of Balzac's not merely his failure ever to attain, except in passages and patches, a thoroughly great style, but also that extraordinary method of composition which in after days cost him and his publishers so much money.

However, if these ten years of probation taught him his trade, they taught him also a most unfortunate avocation or by-trade, which he never ceased to practise, or to try to practise, which never did him the least good, and which not unfrequently lost him much of the not too abundant gains which he earned with such enormous labor. This was the "game of speculation." His sister puts the tempter's part on an unknown "neighbor," who advised him to try to procure independence by *une bonne spéculation*. Those who have read Balzac's books and his letters will hardly think that he required much tempting. He began by trying to publish—an attempt which has never yet succeeded with a single man of letters, so far as I can remember. His scheme was not a bad one, indeed it was one which has brought much money to other pockets since, being neither more nor less than the issuing of cheap one-volume editions of French classics. But he had hardly any capital; he was naturally quite ignorant of his trade, and as naturally the established publishers and booksellers boycotted him as an intruder. So his *Moliere* and his *La Fontaine* are said to have been sold as waste paper, though if any copies escaped they would probably fetch a very comfortable price now. Then, such capital as he had having been borrowed, the lender, either out of good nature or avarice, determined to throw the helve after the hatchet. He partly advanced himself and partly induced Balzac's parents to advance more, in order to start the young man as a printer, to which business Honore himself added that of typefounder. The story was just the same: knowledge and capital were again wanting, and though actual bankruptcy was avoided, Balzac got out of the matter at the cost not merely of giving the two businesses to a friend (in whose hands they proved profitable), but of a margin of debt from which he may be said never to have fully cleared himself.

He had more than twenty years to live, but he never cured himself of this hankering after *une bonne speculation*. Sometimes it was ordinary stock-exchange gambling; but his special weakness was, to do him justice, for schemes that had something more grandiose in them. Thus, to finish here with the subject, though the chapter of it never actually finished till his death, he made years afterwards, when he was a successful and a desperately busy author, a long, troublesome, and costly journey to Sardinia to carry out a plan of resmelting the slag from Roman and other mines there. Thus in his very latest days, when he was living at Vierzschovnia with the Hanska and Mniszech household, he conceived the magnificently absurd notion of cutting down twenty thousand acres of oak wood in the Ukraine, and sending it *by railway* right across Europe to be sold in France. And he was rather reluctantly convinced that by the time a single log reached its market the freight would have eaten up the value of the whole plantation.

It was perhaps not entirely chance that the collapse of the printing scheme, which took place in 1827, the ninth year of the Wanderings in the Wilderness, coincided with or immediately preceded the conception of the book which was to give Balzac passage into the Promised Land. This was *Les Chouans*, called at its first issue, which differed considerably from the present form, *Le Dernier Chouan ou la Bretagne en 1800* (later *1799*). It was published in 1829 without any of the previous anagrammatic pseudonyms; and whatever were the reasons which had induced him to make his bow in person to the public, they were well justified, for the book was a distinct success, if not a great one. It occupies a kind of middle position between the melodramatic romance of his nonage and the strictly analytic romance-novel of his later time; and, though dealing with war and love chiefly, inclines in conception distinctly to the latter. Corentin, Hulot, and other personages of the actual Comedy (then by no means planned, or at least avowed) appear; and though the influence of Scott is in a way paramount* on the surface, the underwork is quite different, and the whole scheme of the loves of Montauran and Mademoiselle de Verneuil is pure Balzac.

* Balzac was throughout his life a fervent admirer of Sir Walter, and I think Mr. Wedmore, in his passage on the subject, distinctly undervalues both the character and the duration of this esteem. Balzac was far too acute to commit the common mistake of thinking Scott superficial—men who know mankind are not often blind to each other's knowledge. And while Mr. Wedmore seems not to know any testimony later than Balzac's *thirty-eighth* year, it is in his *forty-sixth*, when all his own best work was done, except the *Parents Pauvres*, that he contrasts Dumas with Scott saying that *on relit Walter Scott*, and he does not think any one will re-read Dumas. This may be unjust to the one writer, but it is conclusive as to any sense of "wasted time" (his own phrase) having ever existed in Balzac's mind about the other.

It would seem as if nothing but this sun of popular approval had been wanting to make Balzac's genius burst out in full bloom. Although we have a fair number of letters for the ensuing years, it is not very easy to make out the exact sequence of production of the marvelous harvest which his genius gave. It is sufficient to say that in the three years following 1829 there were actually published the *Physiologie du Mariage*, the charming story of *La Maison du Chat-que-Pelote*, the *Peau de Chagrin*, the most original and splendid, if not the most finished and refined, of all Balzac's books, most of the short *Contes Philosophiques*, of which some are among their author's greatest triumphs, many other stories (chiefly included in the *Scenes de la Vie Privee*) and the beginning of the *Contes Drolatiques*.*

* No regular attempt will after this be made to indicate the date of production of successive works, unless they connect themselves very distinctly with incidents in the life or with general critical observations. At the end of this introduction will be found a full table of the Comedie Humaine and the other works. It may perhaps be worth while to add here, that while the labors of M. de Lovenjoul (to whom every writer on Balzac must acknowledge the deepest obligation) have cleared this matter up almost to the verge of possibility as regards the published works, there is little light to be thrown on the constant references in the letters to books which never appeared. Sometimes they are known, and they may often be suspected, to have been absorbed into or incorporated with others; the rest must have been lost or destroyed, or, which is not quite impossible, have existed chiefly in the form of project. Nearly a hundred titles of such things are preserved.

But without a careful examination of his miscellaneous work, which is very abundant and includes journalism as well as books, it is almost as impossible to come to a just appreciation of Balzac as it is without reading the early works and letters. This miscellaneous work is all the more important because a great deal of it represents the artist at quite advanced stages of his career, and because all its examples, the earlier as well as the later, give us abundant insight on him as he was "making himself." The comparison with the early works of Thackeray (in *Punch*, *Fraser*, and elsewhere) is so striking that it can escape no one who knows the two. Every now and then Balzac transferred bodily, or with slight alterations, passages from these experiments to his finished canvases. It appears that he had a scheme for codifying his "Physiologies" (of which the notorious one above mentioned is only a catchpenny exemplar and very far from the best) into a seriously organized work. Chance was kind or intention was wise in not allowing him to do so; but the value of the things for the critical reader is not less. Here are tales—extensions of the scheme and manner of the *Oeuvres de Jeunesse*, or attempts at the *goguenard* story of 1830—a thing for which Balzac's hand was hardly light enough. Here are interesting evidences of striving to be cosmopolitan and polyglot—the most interesting of all of which, I think, is the mention of certain British products as "mufflings." "Muffling" used to be a domestic joke for "muffin;" but whether some wicked Briton deluded Balzac into the idea that it was the proper form or not it is impossible to say. Here is a *Traite de la Vie Elegante*, inestimable for certain critical purposes. So early as 1825 we find a *Code des Gens Honnetes*, which exhibits at once the author's legal studies and his constant attraction for the shady side of business, and which contains a scheme for defrauding by means of lead pencils, actually carried out (if we may believe his exulting note) by some literary swindlers with unhappy results. A year later he wrote a *Dictionnaire des Enseignes de Paris*, which we are glad enough to have from the author of the *Chat-que-Pelote*; but the persistence with which this kind of miscellaneous writing occupied him could not be better exemplified than by the fact that, of two important works which closely follow this in the collected edition, the *Physiologie de l'Employe* dates from 1841 and the *Monographie de la Presse Parisienne* from 1843.

It is well known that from the time almost of his success as a novelist he was given, like too many successful novelists *(not* like Scott), to rather undignified and foolish attacks on critics. The explanation may or may not be found in the fact that we have abundant critical work of his, and that it is nearly all bad. Now and then we have an acute remark in his own special sphere; but as a rule he cannot be complimented on these performances, and when he was half-way through his career this critical tendency of his culminated in the unlucky *Revue Parisienne*, which he wrote almost entirely himself, with slight assistance from his friends, MM. de Belloy and de Grammont. It covers a wide range, but the literary part of it is considerable, and this part contains that memorable and disastrous attack on Sainte-Beuve, for which the critic afterwards took a magnanimous revenge in his obituary *causerie*. Although the thing is not quite unexampled it is not easily to be surpassed in the blind fury of its abuse. Sainte-Beuve was by no means invulnerable, and an anti-critic who kept his head might have found, as M. de Pontmartin and others did find, the joints in his armor. But when, *a propos* of the *Port Royal* more especially, and of the other works in general, Balzac informs us that Sainte-Beuve's great characteristic as a writer is *l'ennui, l'ennui boueux jusqu'a mi-jambe*, that his style is intolerable, that his historical handling is like that of Gibbon, Hume, and other dull people; when he jeers at him for exhuming "La mere Angelique," and scolds him for presuming to obscure the glory of the *Roi Soleil*, the thing is partly ludicrous, partly melancholy. One remembers that agreeable Bohemian, who at a symposium once interrupted his host by crying, "Man o' the hoose, gie us less o' yer clack and mair o' yer Jairman wine!" Only, in human respect and other, we phrase it: "Oh, dear M. de Balzac! give us more *Eugenie Grandets*, more *Pere Goriots*, more *Peaux de Chagrin*, and don't talk about what you do not understand!"

Balzac was a great politician also, and here, though he may not have been very much more successful, he talked with more knowledge and competence. He must have given himself immense trouble in reading the papers, foreign as well as French; he had really mastered a good deal of the political religion of a French publicist. It is curious to read, sixty years after date, his grave assertion that *"La France a la conquete de Madagascar a faire,"* and with certain very pardonable defects (such as his Anglophobia), his politics may be pronounced not unintelligent and not ungenerous, though somewhat inconsistent and not very distinctly traceable to any coherent theory. As for the Anglophobia, the Englishman who thinks the less of him for that must have very poor and unhappy brains. A Frenchman who does not more or less hate and fear England, an Englishman who does not regard France with a more or less good-humored impatience, is usually "either a god or a beast," as Aristotle saith. Balzac began with an odd but not unintelligible compound, something like Hugo's, of Napoleonism and Royalism. In 1824, when he was still in the shades of anonymity, he wrote and published two by no means despicable pamphlets in favor of Primogeniture and the Jesuits, the latter of which was reprinted in 1880 at the last *Jesuitenhetze* in France. His *Lettres sur Paris* in 1830-31, and his *La France et l'Etranger* in 1836, are two considerable series of letters from "Our Own Correspondent," handling the affairs of the world with boldness and industry if not invariably with wisdom. They rather suggest (as does the later *Revue Parisienne* still more) the political writing of the age of Anne in England, and perhaps a little later, when "the wits" handled politics and society, literature and things in general with unquestioned competence and an easy universality.

The rest of his work which will not appear in this edition may be conveniently despatched here. The *Physiologie du Mariage* and the *Scenes de la Vie Conjugale* suffer not merely from the most obvious of their faults but from defect of knowledge. It may or may not be that marriage, in the hackneyed phrase, is a net or other receptacle where all the outsiders would be in, and all the insiders out. But it is quite clear that Coelebs cannot talk of it with much authority. His state may or may not be the more gracious: his judgment cannot but lack experience. The "Theatre," which brought the author little if any profit, great annoyance, and a vast amount of trouble, has been generally condemned by criticism. But the *Contes Drolatiques* are not so to be given up. The famous and splendid *Succube* is only the best of them, and though all are more or less tarred with the brush which tars so much of French literature, though the attempt to write in an archaic style is at best a very successful *tour de force*, and represents an expenditure of brain power by no means justifiable on the part of a man who could have made so much better use of it, they are never to be spoken of disrespectfully. Those who sneer at their "Wardour Street" Old French are not usually the best qualified to do so; and it is not to be forgotten that Balzac was a real countryman of Rabelais and a legitimate inheritor of *Gauloiserie*. Unluckily no man can "throw back" in this way, except now and then as a mere pastime. And it is fair to recollect that as a matter of fact Balzac, after a year or two, did not waste much more time on these things, and that the intended ten *dizains* never, as a matter of fact, went beyond three.

Besides this work in books, pamphlets, etc., Balzac, as has been said, did a certain amount of journalism, especially in the *Caricature*, his performances including, I regret to say, more than one puff of his own work; and in this, as well as by the success of the *Chouans*, he became known about 1830 to a much wider circle, both of literary and of private acquaintance. It cannot indeed be said that he ever mixed much in society; it was impossible that he should do so, considering the vast amount of work he did and the manner in which he did it. This subject, like that of his speculations, may be better finished off in a single passage than dealt with by scattered indications here and there. He was not one of those men who can do work by fits and starts in the intervals of business or of amusement; nor was he one who, like Scott, could work very rapidly. It is true that he often achieved immense quantities of work (subject to a caution to be given presently) in a very few days, but then his working day was of the most peculiar character. He could not bear disturbance; he wrote best at night, and he could not work at all after heavy meals. His favorite plan (varied sometimes in detail) was therefore to dine lightly about five or six, then to go to bed and sleep till eleven, twelve, or one, and then to get up, and with the help only of coffee (which he drank very strong and in enormous quantities) to work for indefinite stretches of time into the morning or afternoon of the next day. He speaks of a sixteen hours' day as a not uncommon shift or spell of work, and almost a regular one with him; and on one occasion he avers that in the course of forty-eight hours he took but three of the rest, working for twenty-two hours and a half continuously on each side thereof. In such spells, supposing reasonable facility of composition and mechanical power in the hand to keep going all the time, an enormous amount can of course be accomplished. A thousand words an hour is anything but an extraordinary rate of writing, and fifteen hundred by no means unheard of with persons who do not write rubbish.

The references to this subject in Balzac's letters are very numerous; but it is not easy to extract very definite information from them. It would be not only impolite but incorrect to charge him with unveracity. But the very heat of imagination which enabled him to produce his work created a sort of mirage, through which he seems always to have regarded it; and in writing to publishers, editors, creditors, and even his own family, it was too obviously his interest to make the most of his labor, his projects, and his performance. Even his contemporary, though elder, Southey, the hardest-working and the most scrupulously honest man of letters in England who could pretend to genius, seems constantly to have exaggerated the idea of what he could perform, if not of what he had performed in a given time. The most definite statement of Balzac's that I remember is one which claims the second number of *Sur Catherine de Medicis*, "La Confidence des Ruggieri," as the production of a single night, and not one of the most extravagant of his nights. Now, "La Confidence des Ruggieri" fills, in the small edition, eighty pages of nearer four hundred than three hundred words each, or some thirty thousand words in all. Nobody in the longest of nights could manage that, except by dictating it to shorthand clerks. But in the very context of this assertion Balzac assigns a much longer period to the correction than to the composition, and this brings us to one of the most curious and one of the most famous points of his literary history.

Some doubts have, I believe, been thrown on the most minute account of his ways of composition which we have, that of the publisher Werdet. But there is too great a consensus of evidence as to his general system to make the received description of it doubtful. According to this, the first draft of Balzac's work never presented it in anything like fulness, and sometimes it did not amount to a quarter of the bulk finally published. This being returned to him from the printer in "slip" on sheets with very large margins, he would set to work on the correction; that is to say, on the practical rewriting of the thing, with excisions, alterations, and above all, additions. A "revise" being executed, he would attack this revise in the same manner, and not unfrequently more than once, so that the expenses of mere composition and correction of the press were enormously heavy (so heavy as to eat into not merely his publisher's but his own profits), and that the last state of the book, when published, was something utterly different from its first state in manuscript. And it will be obvious that if anything like this was usual with him, it is quite impossible to judge his actual rapidity of composition by the extent of the published result.

However this may be (and it is at least certain that in the years above referred to he must have worked his very hardest, even if some of the work then published had been more or less excogitated and begun during the Wilderness period), he certainly so far left his eremitical habits as to become acquainted with most of the great men of letters of the early thirties, and also with certain ladies of more or less high rank, who were to supply, if not exactly the full models, the texts and starting-points for some of the most interesting figures of the *Comedie*. He knew Victor Hugo, but certainly not at this time intimately; for as late as 1839 the letter in which he writes to Hugo to come and breakfast with him at Les Jardies (with interesting and minute directions how to find that frail abode of genius) is couched in anything but the tone of a familiar friendship. The letters to Beyle of about the same date are also incompatible with intimate knowledge. Nodier (after some contrary expressions) he seems to have regarded as most good people did regard that true man of letters and charming tale-teller; while among the younger generation Theophile Gautier and Charles de Bernard, as well as Goslan and others, were his real and constant friends. But he does not figure frequently or eminently in any of the genuine gossip of the time as a haunter of literary circles, and it is very nearly certain that the assiduity with which some of his heroes attend *salons* and clubs had no counterpart in his own life. In the first place he was too busy; in the second he would not have been at home there. Like the young gentleman in *Punch*, who "did not read books but wrote them," though in no satiric sense, he felt it his business not to frequent society but to create it.

He was, however, aided in the task of creation by the ladies already spoken of, who were fairly numerous and of divers degrees. The most constant, after his sister Laure, was that sister's schoolfellow, Madame Zulma Carraud, the wife of a military official at Angouleme and the possessor of a small country estate at Frapesle, near Tours. At both of these places Balzac, till he was a very great man, was a constant visitor, and with Madame Carraud he kept up for years a correspondence which has been held to be merely friendly, and which was certainly in the vulgar sense innocent, but which seems to me to be tinged with something of that feeling, midway between love and friendship, which appears in Scott's letters to Lady Abercorn, and which is probably not so rare as some think. Madame de Berny, another family friend of higher rank, was the prototype of most of his "angelic" characters, but she died in 1836. He knew the Duchesse d'Abrantes, otherwise Madame Junot, and Madame de Girardin, otherwise Delphine Gay; but neither seems to have exercised much influence over him. It was different with another and more authentic duchess, Madame de Castries, after whom he dangled for a considerable time, who certainly first encouraged him and probably then snubbed him, and who is thought to have been the model of his wickeder great ladies. And it was comparatively early in the thirties that he met the woman whom, after nearly twenty years, he was at last to marry, getting his death in so doing, the Polish Madame Hanska. These, with some relations of the last named, especially her daughter, and with a certain "Louise"—an *Inconnue* who never ceased to be so—were Balzac's chief correspondents of the other sex, and, as far as is known, his chief friends in it.

About his life, without extravagant "pudding" of guesswork or of mere quotation and abstract of his letters, it would be not so much difficult as impossible to say much; and accordingly it is a matter of fact that most lives of Balzac, including all good ones, are rather critical than narrative. From his real *debut* with *Le Dernier Chouan* to his departure for Poland on the long visit, or brace of visits, from which he returned finally to die, this life consisted solely of work. One of his earliest utterances, *"Il faut piocher ferme,"* was his motto to the very last, varied only by a certain amount of traveling. Balzac was always a considerable traveler; indeed if he had not been so his constitution would probably have broken down long before it actually did; and the expense of these voyagings (though by his own account he generally conducted his affairs with the most rigid economy), together with the interruption to his work which they occasioned, entered no doubt for something into his money difficulties. He would go to Baden or Vienna for a day's sight of Madame Hanska; his Sardinian visit has been already noted; and as a specimen of others it may be mentioned that he once journeyed from Paris to Besancon, then from Besancon right across France to Angouleme, and then back to Paris on some business of selecting paper for one of the editions of his books, which his publishers would probably have done much better and at much less expense.

Still his actual receipts were surprisingly small, partly, it may be, owing to his expensive habits of composition, but far more, according to his own account, because of the Belgian piracies, from which all popular French authors suffered till the government of Napoleon the Third managed to put a stop to them. He also lived in such a thick atmosphere of bills and advances and cross-claims on and by his publishers, that even if there were more documents than there are it would be exceedingly difficult to get at facts which are, after all, not very important. He never seems to have been paid much more than 500 pounds for the newspaper publication (the most valuable by far because the pirates could not interfere with its profits) of any one of his novels. And to expensive fashions of composition and complicated accounts, a steady back-drag of debt and the rest, must be added the very delightful, and to the novelist not useless, but very expensive mania for the collector. Balzac had a genuine taste for, and thought himself a genuine connoisseur in, pictures, sculpture, and objects of art of all kinds, old and new; and though prices in his day were not what they are in these, a great deal of money must have run through his hands in this way. He calculated the value of the contents of the house, which in his last days he furnished with such loving care for his wife, and which turned out to be a chamber rather of death than of marriage, at some 16,000 pounds. But part of this was Madame Hanska's own purchasing, and there were offsets of indebtedness against it almost to the last. In short, though during the last twenty years of his life such actual "want of pence" as vexed him was not due, as it had been earlier, to the fact that the pence refused to come in, but only to imprudent management of them, it certainly cannot be said that Honore de Balzac, the most desperately hard worker in all literature for such time as was allotted him, and perhaps the man of greatest genius who was ever a desperately hard worker, falsified that most uncomfortable but truest of proverbs—"Hard work never made money."

If, however, he was but scantily rewarded with the money for which he had a craving (not absolutely, I think, devoid of a touch of genuine avarice, but consisting chiefly of the artist's desire for pleasant and beautiful things, and partly presenting a variety or phase of the grandiose imagination, which was his ruling characteristic), Balzac had plenty of the fame, for which he cared quite as much as he cared for money. Perhaps no writer except Voltaire and Goethe earlier made such a really European reputation; and his books were of a kind to be more widely read by the general public than either Goethe's or Voltaire's. In England (Balzac liked the literature but not the country, and never visited England, though I believe he planned a visit) this popularity was, for obvious reasons, rather less than elsewhere. The respectful vogue which French literature had had with the English in the eighteenth century had ceased, owing partly to the national enmity revived and fostered by the great war, and partly to the growth of a fresh and magnificent literature at home during the first thirty years of the nineteenth in England. But Balzac could not fail to be read almost at once by the lettered; and he was translated pretty early, though not perhaps to any great extent. It was in England, moreover, that by far his greatest follower appeared, and appeared very shortly. For it would be absurd in the most bigoted admirer of Thackeray to deny that the author of *Vanity Fair*, who was in Paris and narrowly watching French literature and French life at the very time of Balzac's most exuberant flourishing and education, owed something to the author of *Le Pere Goriot*. There was no copying or imitation; the lessons taught by Balzac were too much blended with those of native masters, such as Fielding, and too much informed and transformed by individual genius. Some may think—it is a point at issue not merely between Frenchmen and Englishmen, but between good judges of both nations on each side—that in absolute veracity and likeness to life, in limiting the operation of the inner consciousness on the outward observation to strictly artistic scale, Thackeray excelled Balzac as far as he fell short of him in the powers of the seer and in the gigantic imagination of the prophet. But the relations of pupil and master in at least some degree are not, I think, deniable.

So things went on in light and in shade, in homekeeping and in travel, in debts and in earnings, but always in work of some kind or another, for eighteen years from the turning point of 1829. By degrees, as he gained fame and ceased to be in the most pressing want of money, Balzac left off to some extent, though never entirely, those miscellaneous writings—reviews (including puffs), comic or general sketches, political diatribes, "physiologies" and the like— which, with his discarded prefaces and much more interesting matter, were at last, not many years ago, included in four stout volumes of the *Edition Definitive*. With the exception of the *Physiologies* (a sort of short satiric analysis of this or that class, character, or personage), which were very popular in the reign of Louis Philippe in France, and which Albert Smith and others introduced into

England, Balzac did not do any of this miscellaneous work extremely well. Very shrewd observations are to be found in his reviews, for instance his indication, in reviewing La Touche's *Fragoletta*, of that common fault of ambitious novels, a sort of woolly and "ungraspable" looseness of construction and story, which constantly bewilders the reader as to what is going on. But, as a rule, he was thinking too much of his own work and his own principles of working to enter very thoroughly into the work of others. His politics, those of a moderate but decided Royalist and Conservative, were, as has been said, intelligent in theory, but in practice a little distinguished by that neglect of actual business detail which has been noticed in his speculations.

At last, in the summer of 1847, it seemed as if the Rachel for whom he had served nearly if not quite the full fourteen years already, and whose husband had long been out of the way, would at last grant herself to him. He was invited to Vierzschovnia in the Ukraine, the seat of Madame Hanska, or in strictness of her son-in-law, Count Georges Mniszech; and as the visit was apparently for no restricted period, and Balzac's pretensions to the lady's hand were notorious, it might have seemed that he was as good as accepted. But to assume this would have been to mistake what perhaps the greatest creation of Balzac's great English contemporary and counterpart on the one side, as Thackeray was his contemporary and counterpart on the other, considered to be the malignity of widows. What the reasons were which made Madame Hanska delay so long in doing what she did at last, and might just as well, it would seem, have done years before, is not certainly known, and it would be quite unprofitable to discuss them. But it was on the 8th of October 1847 that Balzac first wrote to his sister from Vierzschovnia, and it was not till the 14th of March 1850 that, "in the parish church of Saint Barbara at Berditchef, by the Count Abbe Czarski, representing the Bishop of Jitomir (this is as characteristic of Balzac in one way as what follows is in another) a Madame Eve de Balzac, born Countess Rzevuska, or a Madame Honore de Balzac or a Madame de Balzac the elder" came into existence.

It does not appear that Balzac was exactly unhappy during this huge probation, which was broken by one short visit to Paris. The interest of uncertainty was probably much for his ardent and unquiet spirit, and though he did very little literary work for him, one may suspect that he would not have done very much if he had stayed at Paris, for signs of exhaustion, not of genius but of physical power, had shown themselves before he left home. But it is not unjust or cruel to say that by the delay "Madame Eve de Balzac" (her actual baptismal name was Evelina) practically killed her husband. These winters in the severe climate of Russian Poland were absolutely fatal to a constitution, and especially to lungs, already deeply affected. At Vierzschovnia itself he had illnesses, from which he narrowly escaped with life, before the marriage; his heart broke down after it; and he and his wife did not reach Paris till the end of May. Less than three months afterwards, on the 18th of August, he died, having been visited on the very day of his death in the Paradise of bric-a-brac which he had created for his Eve in the Rue Fortunee—a name too provocative of Nemesis—by Victor Hugo, the chief maker in verse as he himself was the chief maker in prose of France. He was buried at Pere la Chaise. The after-fortunes of his house and its occupants were not happy: but they do not concern us.

In person Balzac was a typical Frenchman, as indeed he was in most ways. From his portraits there would seem to have been more force and address than distinction or refinement in his appearance, but, as has been already observed, his period was one ungrateful to the iconographer. His character, not as a writer but as a man, must occupy us a little longer. For some considerable time—indeed it may be said until the publication of his letters—it was not very favorably judged on the whole. We may, of course, dismiss the childish scandals (arising, as usual, from clumsy or malevolent misinterpretation of such books as the *Physiologie de Mariage*, the *Peau de Chagrin*, and a few others), which gave rise to the caricatures of him such as that of which we read, representing him in a monk's dress at a table covered with bottles and supporting a young person on his knee, the whole garnished with the epigraph: Scenes de la Vie Cachee. They seem to have given him, personally, a very unnecessary annoyance, and indeed he was always rather sensitive to criticism. This kind of stupid libel will never cease to be devised by the envious, swallowed by the vulgar, and simply neglected by the wise. But Balzac's peculiarities, both of life and of work, lent themselves rather fatally to a subtler misconstruction which he also anticipated and tried to remove, but which took a far stronger hold. He was represented—and in the absence of any intimate male friends to contradict the representation, it was certain to obtain some currency—as in his artistic person a sardonic libeler of mankind, who cared only to take foibles and vices for his subjects, and who either left goodness and virtue out of sight altogether, or represented them as the qualities of fools. In private life he was held up as at the best a self-centered egotist who cared for nothing but himself and his own work, capable of interrupting one friend who told him of the death of a sister by the suggestion that they should change the subject and talk of "something real, of *Eugenie Grandet*," and of levying a fifty per cent commission on another who had written a critical notice of his, Balzac's, life and works.*

* Sandeau and Gautier, the victims in these two stories, were neither spiteful, nor mendacious, nor irrational, so they are probably true. The second was possibly due to Balzac's odd notions of "business being business." The first, I have quite recently seen reason to think, may have been a sort of reminiscence of one of the traits in Diderot's extravagant encomium on Richardson.

With the first of these charges he himself, on different occasions, rather vainly endeavored to grapple, once drawing up an elaborate list of his virtuous and vicious women, and showing that the former outnumbered the latter; and, again, laboring (with that curious lack of sense of humor which distinguishes all Frenchmen but a very few, and distinguished him eminently) to show that though no doubt it is very difficult to make a virtuous person interesting, he, Honore de Balzac, had attempted it, and succeeded in it, on a quite surprising number of occasions.

The fact is that if he had handled this last matter rather more lightly his answer would have been a sufficient one, and that in any case the charge is not worth answering. It does not lie against the whole of his work; and if it lay as conclusively as it does against Swift's, it would not necessarily matter. To the artist in analysis as opposed to the romance-writer, folly always, and villainy sometimes, does supply a much better subject than virtuous success, and if he makes his fools and his villains lifelike and supplies them with a fair contrast of better things, there is nothing more to be said. He will not, indeed, be a Shakespeare, or a Dante, or even a Scott; but we may be very well satisfied with him as a Fielding, a Thackeray, or a Balzac. As to the more purely personal matter I own that it was some time before I could persuade myself that Balzac, to speak familiarly, was a much better fellow than others, and I myself, have been accustomed to think him. But it is also some time since I came to the conclusion that he was so, and my conversion is not to be attributed to any editorial retainer. His education in a lawyer's office, the accursed advice about the *bonne speculation*, and his constant straitenings for money, will account for his sometimes looking after the main chance rather too narrowly; and as for the Eugenie Grandet story (even if the supposition referred to in a note above be fanciful) it requires no great stretch of charity or comprehension to see in it nothing more awkward, very easily misconstrued, but not necessarily in the least heartless or brutal attempt of a rather absent and very much self-centered recluse absorbed in one subject, to get his interlocutor as well as himself out of painful and useless dwelling on sorrowful matters. Self-centered and self-absorbed Balzac no doubt was; he could not have lived his life or produced his work if he had been anything else. And it must be remembered that he owed extremely little to others; that he had the independence as well as the isolation of the self-centered; that he never sponged or fawned on a great man, or wronged others of what was due to them. The only really unpleasant thing about him that I know, and even this is perhaps due to ignorance of all sides of the matter, is a slight touch of snobbishness now and then, especially in those late letters from Vierzschovnia to Madame de Balzac and Madame Surville, in which, while inundating his mother and sister with commissions and requests for service, he points out to them what great people the Hanskas and Mniszechs are, what infinite honor and profit it will be to be connected with them, and how desirable it is to keep struggling engineer brothers-in-law and ne'er-do-well brothers in the colonies out of sight lest they should disgust the magnates.

But these are "sma' sums, sma' sums," as Bailie Jarvie says; and smallness of any kind has, whatever it may have to do with Balzac the man, nothing to do with Balzac the writer. With him as with some others, but not as with the larger number, the sense of *greatness* increases the longer and the more fully he is studied. He resembles, I think, Goethe more than any other man of letters—certainly more than any other of the present century—in having done work which is very frequently, if not even commonly, faulty, and in yet requiring that his work shall be known as a whole. His appeal is cumulative; it repeats itself on each occasion with a slight difference, and though there may now and then be the same faults to be noticed, they are almost invariably accompanied, not merely by the same, but by fresh merits.

As has been said at the beginning of this essay, no attempt will be made in it to give that running survey of Balzac's work which is always useful and sometimes indispensable in treatment of the kind. But something like a summing up of that subject will here be attempted because it is really desirable that in embarking on so vast a voyage the reader should have some general chart—some notes of the soundings and log generally of those who have gone before him.

There are two things, then, which it is more especially desirable to keep constantly before one in reading Balzac—two things which, taken together, constitute his almost unique value, and two things which not a few critics have failed to take together in him, being under the impression that the one excludes the other, and that to admit the other is tantamount to a denial of the one. These two things are, first, an immense attention to detail, sometimes observed, sometimes invented or imagined; and secondly; a faculty of regarding these details through a mental lens or arrangement of lenses almost peculiar to himself, which at once combines, enlarges, and invests them with a peculiar magical halo or mirage. The two thousand personages of the *Comedie Humaine* are, for the most part, "signaled," as the French official word has it, marked and denoted by the minutest traits of character, gesture, gait, clothing, abode, what not; the transactions recorded are very often given with a scrupulous and microscopic accuracy of reporting which no detective could outdo. Defoe is not more circumstantial in detail of fact than Balzac; Richardson is hardly more prodigal of character-stroke. Yet a very large proportion of these characters, of these circumstances, are evidently things invented or imagined, not observed. And in addition to this the artist's magic glass, his Balzacian speculum, if we may so say (for none else has ever had it), transforms even the most rigid observation into something flickering and fanciful, the outline as of shadows on the wall, not the precise contour of etching or of the camera.

It is curious, but not unexampled, that both Balzac himself when he struggled in argument with his critics and those of his partisans who have been most zealously devoted to him, have usually tried to exalt the first and less remarkable of these gifts over the second and infinitely more remarkable. Balzac protested strenuously against the use of the word "gigantesque" in reference to his work; and of course it is susceptible of an unhandsome innuendo. But if we leave that innuendo aside, if we adopt the sane reflection that "gigantesque" does not exceed "gigantic," or assert as constant failure of greatness, but only indicates that the magnifying process is carried on with a certain indiscriminateness, we shall find none, I think, which so thoroughly well describes him.

The effect of this singular combination of qualities, apparently the most opposite, may be partly anticipated, but not quite. It results occasionally in a certain shortcoming as regards *verite vraie*, absolute artistic truth to nature. Those who would range Balzac in point of such artistic veracity on a level with poetical and universal realists like Shakespeare and Dante, or prosaic and particular realists like Thackeray and Fielding, seem not only to be utterly wrong but to pay their idol the worst of all compliments, that of ignoring his own special qualifications. The province of Balzac may not be—I do no think it is—identical, much less co-extensive, with that of nature. But it is his own—a partly real, partly fantastic region, where the lights, the shades, the dimensions, and the physical laws are slightly different from those of this world of ours, but with which, owing to the things it has in common with that world, we are able to sympathize, which we can traverse and comprehend. Every now and then the artist uses his observing faculty more, and his magnifying and distorting lens less; every now and then he reverses the proportion. Some tastes will like him best in the one stage; some in the other; the happier constituted will like him best in both. These latter will decline to put *Eugenie Grandet* above the *Peau de Chagrin*, or *Le Pere Goriot* above the wonderful handful of tales which includes *La Recherche de l'Absolu* and *Le Chef-d'oeuvre Inconnu*, though they will no doubt recognize that even in the first two named members of these pairs the Balzacian quality, that of magnifying and rendering grandiose, is present, and that the martyrdom of Eugenie, the avarice of her father, the blind self-devotion of Goriot to his thankless and worthless children, would not be what they are if they were seen through a perfectly achromatic and normal medium.

This specially Balzacian quality is, I think, unique. It is like—it may almost be said to *be*—the poetic imagination, present in magnificent volume and degree, but in some miraculous way deprived and sterilized of the specially poetical quality. By this I do not of course mean that Balzac did not write in verse: we have a few verses of his, and they are pretty bad, but that is neither here nor there. The difference between Balzac and a great poet lies not in the fact that the one fills the whole page with printed words, and the other only a part of it—but in something else. If I could put that something else into distinct words I should therein attain the philosopher's stone, the elixir of life, the *primum mobile*, the *grand arcanum*, not merely of criticism but of all things. It might be possible to coast about it, to hint at it, by adumbrations and in consequences.

But it is better and really more helpful to face the difficulty boldly, and to say that Balzac, approaching a great poet nearer perhaps than any other prose writer in any language, is distinguished from one by the absence of the very last touch, the finally constituting quiddity, which makes a great poet different from Balzac.

Now, when we make this comparison, it is of the first interest to remember—and it is one of the uses of the comparison, that it suggests the remembrance of the fact—that the great poets have usually been themselves extremely exact observers of detail. It has not made them great poets; but they would not be great poets without it. And when Eugenie Grandet starts from *le petit banc de bois* at the reference to it in her scoundrelly cousin's letter (to take only one instance out of a thousand), we see in Balzac the same observation, subject to the limitation just mentioned, that we see in Dante and Shakespeare, in Chaucer and Tennyson. But the great poets do not as a rule *accumulate* detail. Balzac does, and from this very accumulation he manages to derive that singular gigantesque vagueness—differing from the poetic vague, but ranking next to it—which I have here ventured to note as his distinguishing quality. He bewilders us a very little by it, and he gives us the impression that he has slightly bewildered himself. But the compensations of the bewilderment are large.

For in this labyrinth and whirl of things, in this heat and hurry of observation and imagination, the special intoxication of Balzac consists. Every great artist has his own means of producing this intoxication, and it differs in result like the stimulus of beauty or of wine. Those persons who are unfortunate enough to see in Balzac little or nothing but an ingenious piler-up of careful strokes—a man of science taking his human documents and classing them after an orderly fashion in portfolio and deed-box—must miss this intoxication altogether. It is much more agreeable as well as much more accurate to see in the manufacture of the *Comedie* the process of a Cyclopean workshop—the bustle, the hurry, the glare and shadow, the steam and sparks of Vulcanian forging. The results, it is true, are by no means confused or disorderly—neither were those of the forges that worked under Lipari—but there certainly went much more to them than the dainty fingering of a literary fretwork-maker or the dull rummagings of a realist *a la Zola*.

In part, no doubt, and in great part, the work of Balzac is dream-stuff rather than life-stuff, and it is all the better for that. What is better than dreams?

But the coherence of his visions, their bulk, their solidity, the way in which they return to us and we return to them, make them such dream-stuff as there is all too little of in this world. If it is true that evil on the whole predominates over good in the vision of this "Voyant," as Philarete Chasles so justly called him, two very respectable, and in one case very large, though somewhat opposed divisions of mankind, the philosophic pessimist and the convinced and consistent Christian believer, will tell us that this is at least not one of the points in which it is unfaithful to life. If the author is closer and more faithful in his study of meanness and vice than in his studies of nobility and virtue, the blame is due at least as much to his models as to himself. If he has seldom succeeded in combining a really passionate with a really noble conception of love, very few of his countrymen have been more fortunate in that respect. If in some of his types—his journalists, his married women, and others—he seems to have sacrificed to conventions, let us remember that those who know attribute to his conventions such a power if not altogether such a holy influence that two generations of the people he painted have actually lived more and more up to his painting of them.

And last of all, but also greatest, has to be considered the immensity of his imaginative achievement, the huge space that he has filled for us with vivid creation, the range of amusement, of instruction, of (after a fashion) edification which he has thrown open for us all to walk in. It is possible that he himself and others more or less well-meaningly, though more or less maladroitly, following his lead, may have exaggerated the coherence and the architectural design of the *Comedie*. But it has coherence and it has design; nor shall we find anything exactly to parallel it. In mere bulk the *Comedie* probably, if not certainly, exceeds the production of any novelist of the first class in any kind of fiction except Dumas, and with Dumas, for various and well-known reasons, there is no possibility of comparing it. All others yield in bulk; all in a certain concentration and intensity; none even aims at anything like the same system and completeness. It must be remembered that owing to shortness of life, lateness of beginning, and the diversion of the author to other work, the *Comedie* is the production, and not the sole production, of some seventeen or eighteen years at most. Not a volume of it, for all that failure to reach the completest perfection in form and style which has been acknowledged, can be accused of thinness, of scamped work, of mere repetition, of mere cobbling up. Every one bears the marks of steady and ferocious labor, as well as of the genius which had at last come where it had been so earnestly called and had never gone away again. It is possible to overpraise Balzac in parts or to mispraise him as a whole. But so long as inappropriate and superfluous comparisons are avoided and as his own excellence is recognized and appreciated, it is scarcely possible to overestimate that excellence in itself and for itself. He stands alone; even with Dickens, who is his nearest analogue, he shows far more points of difference than of likeness. His vastness of bulk is not more remarkable than his peculiarity of quality; and when these two things coincide in literature or elsewhere, then that in which they coincide may be called, and must be called, Great, without hesitation and without reserve.

GEORGE SAINTSBURY.

APPENDIX

THE BALZAC PLAN OF THE COMEDIE HUMAINE

The form in which the Comedie Humaine was left by its author, with the exceptions of *Le Depute d'Arcis* (incomplete) and *Les Petits Bourgeois*, both of which were added, some years later, by the Edition Definitive.

The original French titles are followed by their English equivalents. Literal translations have been followed, excepting a few instances where preference is shown for a clearer or more comprehensive English title.

[Note from Team Balzac, the Etext preparers: In some cases more than one English translation is commonly used for various translations/ editions. In such cases the first translation is from the Saintsbury edition copyrighted in 1901 and that is the title referred to in the personages following most of the stories. We have added other title translations of which we are currently aware for the readers' convenience.]

COMEDIE HUMAINE

SCENES DE LA VIE PRIVEE
SCENES FROM PRIVATE LIFE

La Maison du Chat-qui Pelote
At the Sign of the Cat and Racket

Le Bal de Sceaux
The Ball at Sceaux

La Bourse
The Purse

La Vendetta
The Vendetta

Mme. Firmiani
Madame Firmiani

Une Double Famille
A Second Home

La Paix du Menage
Domestic Peace

La Fausse Maitresse
The Imaginary Mistress
Paz

Etude de femme
A Study of Woman

Autre etude de femme
Another Study of Woman

La Grande Breteche
La Grand Breteche

Albert Savarus
Albert Savarus

Memoires de deux Jeunes Mariees
Letters of Two Brides

Une Fille d'Eve

A Daughter of Eve

La Femme de Trente Ans
A Woman of Thirty

La Femme abandonnee
The Deserted Woman

La Grenadiere
La Grenadiere

Le Message
The Message

Gobseck
Gobseck

Le Contrat de Mariage
A Marriage Settlement
A Marriage Contract

Un Debut dans la vie
A Start in Life

Modeste Mignon
Modeste Mignon

Beatrix
Beatrix

Honorine
Honorine

Le Colonel Chabert
Colonel Chabert

La Messe de l'Athee
The Atheist's Mass

L'Interdiction
The Commission in Lunacy

Pierre Grassou
Pierre Grassou

SCENES DE LA VIE PROVINCE
SCENES FROM PROVINCIAL LIFE

Ursule Mirouet
Ursule Mirouet

Eugenie Grandet
Eugenie Grandet

Les Celibataires:
The Celibates:
    Pierrette
    Pierrette

    Le Cure de Tours
    The Vicar of Tours

Un Menage de Garcon
A Bachelor's Establishment
The Two Brothers
The Black Sheep
La Rabouilleuse

Les Parisiens en Province:
Parisians in the Country:
    L'illustre Gaudissart

Gaudissart the Great
The Illustrious Gaudissart

La Muse du departement
The Muse of the Department

Les Rivalites:
The Jealousies of a Country Town:
   La Vieille Fille
   The Old Maid

   Le Cabinet des antiques
   The Collection of Antiquities

Le Lys dans la Vallee
The Lily of the Valley

Illusions Perdues:—I.
Lost Illusions:—I.
   Les Deux Poetes
   The Two Poets

   Un Grand homme de province a Paris, 1re partie
   A Distinguished Provincial at Paris, Part 1

Illusions Perdues:—II.
Lost Illusions:—II.
   Un Grand homme de province, 2e p.
   A Distinguished Provincial at Paris, Part 2

   Eve et David
   Eve and David

SCENES DE LA VIE PARISIENNE
SCENES FROM PARISIAN LIFE

Splendeurs et Miseres des Courtisanes:
Scenes from a Courtesan's Life:
    Esther heureuse
    Esther Happy

    A combien l'amour revient aux vieillards
    What Love Costs an Old Man

    Ou menent les mauvais Chemins
    The End of Evil Ways

    La derniere Incarnation de Vautrin
    Vautrin's Last Avatar

Un Prince de la Boheme
A Prince of Bohemia

Un Homme d'affaires
A Man of Business

Gaudissart II.
Gaudissart II.

Les Comediens sans le savoir
The Unconscious Humorists
The Unconscious Comedians

Histoire des Treize:
The Thirteen:
    Ferragus
    Ferragus

        La Duchesse de Langeais
        The Duchesse de Langeais

        La Fille aux yeux d'or
        The Girl with the Golden Eyes

Le Pere Goriot
Father Goriot
Old Goriot

Grandeur et Decadence de Cesar Birotteau
The Rise and Fall of Cesar Birotteau

La Maison Nucingen
The Firm of Nucingen

Les Secrets de la princesse de Cadignan
The Secrets of a Princess
The Secrets of the Princess Cadignan

Les Employes
The Government Clerks
Bureaucracy

Sarrasine
Sarrasine

Facino Cane
Facine Cane

Les Parents Pauvres:—I.
Poor Relations:—I.
    La Cousine Bette
    Cousin Betty

Les Parents Pauvres:—II.
Poor Relations:—II.
    Le Cousin Pons
    Cousin Pons

Les Petits Bourgeois
The Middle Classes
The Lesser Bourgeoise

SCENES DE LA VIE POLITIQUE
SCENES FROM POLITICAL LIFE

Une Tenebreuse Affaire
The Gondreville Mystery
An Historical Mystery

Un Episode sous la Terreur
An Episode Under the Terror

L'Envers de l'Histoire Contemporaine:
The Seamy Side of History:
The Brotherhood of Consolation:
    Mme. de la Chanterie
    Madame de la Chanterie

L'Initie
Initiated
The Initiate

Z. Marcas
Z. Marcas

Le Depute d'Arcis
The Member for Arcis
The Deputy for Arcis

SCENES DE LA VIE MILITAIRE
SCENES FROM MILITARY LIFE

Les Chouans
The Chouans

Une Passion dans le desert
A Passion in the Desert

SCENES DE LA VIE DE CAMPAGNE
SCENES FROM COUNTRY LIFE

Le Medecin de Campagne
The Country Doctor

Le Cure de Village
The Country Parson
The Village Rector

Les Paysans
The Peasantry
Sons of the Soil

ETUDES PHILOSOPHIQUES
PHILOSOPHICAL STUDIES

La Peau de Chagrin
The Magic Skin

La Recherche de l'Absolu
The Quest of the Absolute
The Alkahest

Jesus-Christ en Flandre
Christ in Flanders

Melmoth reconcilie
Melmoth Reconciled

Le Chef-d'oeuvre inconnu
The Unknown Masterpiece
The Hidden Masterpiece

L'Enfant Maudit
The Hated Son

Gambara
Gambara

Massimilla Doni
Massimilla Doni

Les Marana
The Maranas
Juana

Adieu
Farewell

Le Requisitionnaire
The Conscript
The Recruit

El Verdugo
El Verdugo

Un Drame au bord de la mer
A Seaside Tragedy
A Drama on the Seashore

L'Auberge rouge
The Red Inn

L'Elixir de longue vie
The Elixir of Life

Maitre Cornelius
Maitre Cornelius

Sur Catherine de Medicis:
About Catherine de' Medici
    Le Martyr calviniste
    The Calvinist Martyr

    La Confidence des Ruggieri
    The Ruggieri's Secret

    Les Deux Reves
    The Two Dreams

Louis Lambert
Louis Lambert

Les Proscrits
The Exiles

Seraphita
Seraphita

AUTHOR'S INTRODUCTION

In giving the general title of "The Human Comedy" to a work begun nearly thirteen years since, it is necessary to explain its motive, to relate its origin, and briefly sketch its plan, while endeavoring to speak of these matters as though I had no personal interest in them. This is not so difficult as the public might imagine. Few works conduce to much vanity; much labor conduces to great diffidence. This observation accounts for the study of their own works made by Corneille, Moliere, and other great writers; if it is impossible to equal them in their fine conceptions, we may try to imitate them in this feeling.

The idea of *The Human Comedy* was at first as a dream to me, one of those impossible projects which we caress and then let fly; a chimera that gives us a glimpse of its smiling woman's face, and forthwith spreads its wings and returns to a heavenly realm of phantasy. But this chimera, like many another, has become a reality; has its behests, its tyranny, which must be obeyed.

The idea originated in a comparison between Humanity and Animality.

It is a mistake to suppose that the great dispute which has lately made a stir, between Cuvier and Geoffroi Saint-Hilaire, arose from a scientific innovation. Unity of structure, under other names, had occupied the greatest minds during the two previous centuries. As we read the extraordinary writings of the mystics who studied the sciences in their relation to infinity, such as Swedenborg, Saint-Martin, and others, and the works of the greatest authors on Natural History—Leibnitz, Buffon, Charles Bonnet, etc., we detect in the *monads* of Leibnitz, in the *organic molecules* of Buffon, in the *vegetative force* of Needham, in the correlation of similar organs of Charles Bonnet—who in 1760 was so bold as to write, "Animals vegetate as plants do"—we detect, I say, the rudiments of the great law of Self for Self, which lies at the root of *Unity of Plan*. There is but one Animal. The Creator works on a single model for every organized being. "The Animal" is elementary, and takes its external form, or, to be accurate, the differences in its form, from the environment in which it is obliged to develop.

Zoological species are the result of these differences. The announcement and defence of this system, which is indeed in harmony with our preconceived ideas of Divine Power, will be the eternal glory of Geoffroi Saint-Hilaire, Cuvier's victorious opponent on this point of higher science, whose triumph was hailed by Goethe in the last article he wrote.

I, for my part, convinced of this scheme of nature long before the discussion to which it has given rise, perceived that in this respect society resembled nature. For does not society modify Man, according to the conditions in which he lives and acts, into men as manifold as the species in Zoology? The differences between a soldier, an artisan, a man of business, a lawyer, an idler, a student, a statesman, a merchant, a sailor, a poet, a beggar, a priest, are as great, though not so easy to define, as those between the wolf, the lion, the ass, the crow, the shark, the seal, the sheep, etc. Thus social species have always existed, and will always exist, just as there are zoological species. If Buffon could produce a magnificent work by attempting to represent in a book the whole realm of zoology, was there not room for a work of the same kind on society? But the limits set by nature to the variations of animals have no existence in society. When Buffon describes the lion, he dismisses the lioness with a few phrases; but in society a wife is not always the female of the male. There may be two perfectly dissimilar beings in one household. The wife of a shopkeeper is sometimes worthy of a prince, and the wife of a prince is often worthless compared with the wife of an artisan. The social state has freaks which Nature does not allow herself; it is nature *plus* society. The description of social species would thus be at least double that of animal species, merely in view of the two sexes. Then, among animals the drama is limited; there is scarcely any confusion; they turn and rend each other—that is all. Men, too, rend each other; but their greater or less intelligence makes the struggle far more complicated. Though some savants do not yet admit that the animal nature flows into human nature through an immense tide of life, the grocer certainly becomes a peer, and the noble sometimes sinks to the lowest social grade. Again, Buffon found that life was extremely simple among animals. Animals have little property, and neither arts nor sciences; while man, by a law that has yet to be sought, has a tendency to express his culture, his thoughts, and his life in everything he appropriates to his use. Though Leuwenhoek, Swammerdam, Spallanzani, Reaumur, Charles Bonnet, Muller, Haller and other patient investigators have shown us how interesting are the habits of animals, those of each kind, are, at least to our eyes, always and in every age alike; whereas the dress, the manners, the speech, the dwelling of a prince, a banker, an artist, a citizen, a priest, and a pauper are absolutely unlike, and change with every phase of civilization.

Hence the work to be written needed a threefold form—men, women, and things; that is to say, persons and the material expression of their minds; man, in short, and life.

As we read the dry and discouraging list of events called History, who can have failed to note that the writers of all periods, in Egypt, Persia, Greece, and Rome, have forgotten to give us a history of manners? The fragment of Petronius on the private life of the Romans excites rather than satisfies our curiosity. It was from observing this great void in the field of history that the Abbe Barthelemy devoted his life to a reconstruction of Greek manners in *Le Jeune Anacharsis*.

But how could such a drama, with the four or five thousand persons which society offers, be made interesting? How, at the same time, please the poet, the philosopher, and the masses who want both poetry and philosophy under striking imagery? Though I could conceive of the importance and of the poetry of such a history of the human heart, I saw no way of writing it; for hitherto the most famous story-tellers had spent their talent in creating two or three typical actors, in depicting one aspect of life. It was with this idea that I read the works of Walter Scott. Walter Scott, the modern troubadour, or finder *(trouvere=trouveur)*, had just then given an aspect of grandeur to a class of composition unjustly regarded as of the second rank. Is it not really more difficult to compete with personal and parochial interests by writing of Daphnis and Chloe, Roland, Amadis, Panurge, Don Quixote, Manon Lescaut, Clarissa, Lovelace, Robinson Crusoe, Gil Blas, Ossian, Julie d'Etanges, My Uncle Toby, Werther, Corinne, Adolphe, Paul and Virginia, Jeanie Deans, Claverhouse, Ivanhoe, Manfred, Mignon, than to set forth in order facts more or less similar in every country, to investigate the spirit of laws that have fallen into desuetude, to review the theories which mislead nations, or, like some metaphysicians, to explain what *Is*? In the first place, these actors, whose existence becomes more prolonged and more authentic than that of the generations which saw their birth, almost always live solely on condition of their being a vast reflection of the present. Conceived in the womb of their own period, the whole heart of humanity stirs within their frame, which often covers a complete system of philosophy. Thus Walter Scott raised to the dignity of the philosophy of History the literature which, from age to age, sets perennial gems in the poetic crown of every nation where letters are cultivated. He vivified it with the spirit of the past; he combined drama, dialogue, portrait, scenery, and description; he fused the marvelous with truth—the two elements of the times; and he brought poetry into close contact with the familiarity of the humblest speech. But as he had not so much devised a system as hit upon a manner in the ardor of his work, or as its logical outcome, he never thought of connecting his compositions in such a way as to form a complete history of which each chapter was a novel, and each novel the picture of a period.

It was by discerning this lack of unity, which in no way detracts from the Scottish writer's greatness, that I perceived at once the scheme which would favor the execution of my purpose, and the possibility of executing it. Though dazzled, so to speak, by Walter Scott's amazing fertility, always himself and always original, I did not despair, for I found the source of his genius in the infinite variety of human nature. Chance is the greatest romancer in the world; we have only to study it. French society would be the real author; I should only be the secretary. By drawing up an inventory of vices and virtues, by collecting the chief facts of the passions, by depicting characters, by choosing the principal incidents of social life, by composing types out of a combination of homogeneous characteristics, I might perhaps succeed in writing the history which so many historians have neglected: that of Manners. By patience and perseverance I might produce for France in the nineteenth century the book which we must all regret that Rome, Athens, Tyre, Memphis, Persia, and India have not bequeathed to us; that history of their social life which, prompted by the Abbe Barthelemy, Monteil patiently and steadily tried to write for the Middle Ages, but in an unattractive form.

This work, so far, was nothing. By adhering to the strict lines of a reproduction a writer might be a more or less faithful, and more or less successful, painter of types of humanity, a narrator of the dramas of private life, an archaeologist of social furniture, a cataloguer of professions, a registrar of good and evil; but to deserve the praise of which every artist must be ambitious, must I not also investigate the reasons or the cause of these social effects, detect the hidden sense of this vast assembly of figures, passions, and incidents? And finally, having sought—I will not say having found—this reason, this motive power, must I not reflect on first principles, and discover in what particulars societies approach or deviate from the eternal law of truth and beauty? In spite of the wide scope of the preliminaries, which might of themselves constitute a book, the work, to be complete, would need a conclusion. Thus depicted, society ought to bear in itself the reason of its working.

The law of the writer, in virtue of which he is a writer, and which I do not hesitate to say makes him the equal, or perhaps the superior, of the statesman, is his judgment, whatever it may be, on human affairs, and his absolute devotion to certain principles. Machiavelli, Hobbes, Bossuet, Leibnitz, Kant, Montesquieu, *are* the science which statesmen apply. "A writer ought to have settled opinions on morals and politics; he should regard himself as a tutor of men; for men need no masters to teach them to doubt," says Bonald. I took these noble words as my guide long ago; they are the written law of the monarchical writer. And those who would confute me by my own words will find that they have misinterpreted some ironical phrase, or that they have turned against me a speech given to one of my actors—a trick peculiar to calumniators.

As to the intimate purpose, the soul of this work, these are the principles on which it is based.

Man is neither good nor bad; he is born with instincts and capabilities; society, far from depraving him, as Rousseau asserts, improves him, makes him better; but self-interest also develops his evil tendencies. Christianity, above all, Catholicism, being—as I have pointed out in the Country Doctor *(le Medecin de Campagne)*—a complete system for the repression of the depraved tendencies of man, is the most powerful element of social order.

In reading attentively the presentment of society cast, as it were, from the life, with all that is good and all that is bad in it, we learn this lesson—if thought, or if passion, which combines thought and feeling, is the vital social element, it is also its destructive element. In this respect social life is like the life of man. Nations live long only by moderating their vital energy. Teaching, or rather education, by religious bodies is the grand principle of life for nations, the only means of diminishing the sum of evil and increasing the sum of good in all society. Thought, the living principle of good and ill, can only be trained, quelled, and guided by religion. The only possible religion is Christianity (see the letter from Paris in "Louis Lambert," in which the young mystic explains, *a propos* to Swedenborg's doctrines, how there has never been but one religion since the world began). Christianity created modern nationalities, and it will preserve them. Hence, no doubt, the necessity for the monarchical principle. Catholicism and Royalty are twin principles.

As to the limits within which these two principles should be confined by various institutions, so that they may not become absolute, every one will feel that a brief preface ought not to be a political treatise. I cannot, therefore, enter on religious discussions, nor on the political discussions of the day. I write under the light of two eternal truths—Religion and Monarchy; two necessities, as they are shown to be by contemporary events, towards which every writer of sound sense ought to try to guide the country back. Without being an enemy to election, which is an excellent principle as a basis of legislation, I reject election regarded as *the only social instrument*, especially so badly organized as it now is (1842); for it fails to represent imposing minorities, whose ideas and interests would occupy the attention of a monarchical government. Elective power extended to all gives us government by the masses, the only irresponsible form of government, under which tyranny is unlimited, for it calls itself law. Besides, I regard the family and not the individual as the true social unit. In this respect, at the risk of being thought retrograde, I side with Bossuet and Bonald instead of going with modern innovators. Since election has become the only social instrument, if I myself were to exercise it no contradiction between my acts and my words should be inferred. An engineer points out that a bridge is about to fall, that it is dangerous for any one to cross it; but he crosses it himself when it is the only road to the town. Napoleon adapted election to the spirit of the French nation with wonderful skill. The least important members of his Legislative Body became the most famous orators of the Chamber after the Restoration. No Chamber has ever been the equal of the *Corps Législatif*, comparing them man for man. The elective system of the Empire was, then, indisputably the best.

Some persons may, perhaps, think that this declaration is somewhat autocratic and self-assertive. They will quarrel with the novelist for wanting to be an historian, and will call him to account for writing politics. I am simply fulfilling an obligation—that is my reply. The work I have undertaken will be as long as a history; I was compelled to explain the logic of it, hitherto unrevealed, and its principles and moral purpose.

Having been obliged to withdraw the prefaces formerly published, in response to essentially ephemeral criticisms, I will retain only one remark.

Writers who have a purpose in view, were it only a reversion to principles familiar in the past because they are eternal, should always clear the ground. Now every one who, in the domain of ideas, brings his stone by pointing out an abuse, or setting a mark on some evil that it may be removed—every such man is stigmatized as immoral. The accusation of immorality, which has never failed to be cast at the courageous writer, is, after all, the last that can be brought when nothing else remains to be said to a romancer. If you are truthful in your pictures; if by dint of daily and nightly toil you succeed in writing the most difficult language in the world, the word *immoral* is flung in your teeth. Socrates was immoral; Jesus Christ was immoral; they both were persecuted in the name of the society they overset or reformed. When a man is to be killed he is taxed with immorality. These tactics, familiar in party warfare, are a disgrace to those who use them. Luther and Calvin knew well what they were about when they shielded themselves behind damaged worldly interests! And they lived all the days of their life.

When depicting all society, sketching it in the immensity of its turmoil, it happened—it could not but happen—that the picture displayed more of evil than of good; that some part of the fresco represented a guilty couple; and the critics at once raised a cry of immorality, without pointing out the morality of another position intended to be a perfect contrast. As the critic knew nothing of the general plan I could forgive him, all the more because one can no more hinder criticism than the use of eyes, tongues, and judgment. Also the time for an impartial verdict is not yet come for me. And, after all, the author who cannot make up his mind to face the fire of criticism should no more think of writing than a traveler should start on his journey counting on a perpetually clear sky. On this point it remains to be said that the most conscientious moralists doubt greatly whether society can show as many good actions as bad ones; and in the picture I have painted of it there are more virtuous figures than reprehensible ones. Blameworthy actions, faults and crimes, from the lightest to the most atrocious, always meet with punishment, human or divine, signal or secret. I have done better than the historian, for I am free. Cromwell here on earth escaped all punishment but that inflicted by thoughtful men. And on this point there have been divided schools. Bossuet even showed some consideration for great regicide. William of Orange, the usurper, Hugues Capet, another usurper, lived to old age with no more qualms or fears than Henri IV. or Charles I. The lives of Catherine II. and of Frederick of Prussia would be conclusive against any kind of moral law, if they were judged by the twofold aspect of the morality which guides ordinary mortals, and that which is in use by crowned heads; for, as Napoleon said, for kings and statesmen there are the lesser and the higher morality. My scenes of political life are founded on this profound observation. It is not a law to history, as it is to romance, to make for a beautiful ideal. History is, or ought to be, what it was; while romance ought to be "the better world," as was said by Mme. Necker, one of the most distinguished thinkers of the last century.

Still, with this noble falsity, romance would be nothing if it were not true in detail. Walter Scott, obliged as he was to conform to the ideas of an essentially hypocritical nation, was false to humanity in his picture of woman, because his models were schismatics. The Protestant woman has no ideal. She may be chaste, pure, virtuous; but her unexpansive love will always be as calm and methodical as the fulfilment of a duty. It might seem as though the Virgin Mary had chilled the hearts of those sophists who have banished her from heaven with her treasures of loving kindness. In Protestantism there is no possible future for the woman who has sinned; while, in the Catholic Church, the hope of forgiveness makes her sublime. Hence, for the Protestant writer there is but one Woman, while the Catholic writer finds a new woman in each new situation. If Walter Scott had been a Catholic, if he had set himself the task of describing truly the various phases of society which have successively existed in Scotland, perhaps the painter of Effie and Alice—the two figures for which he blamed himself in his later years—might have admitted passion with its sins and punishments, and the virtues revealed by repentance. Passion is the sum-total of humanity. Without passion, religion, history, romance, art, would all be useless.

Some persons, seeing me collect such a mass of facts and paint them as they are, with passion for their motive power, have supposed, but wrongly, that I must belong to the school of Sensualism and Materialism—two aspects of the same thing—Pantheism. But their misapprehension was perhaps justified—or inevitable. I do not share the belief in indefinite progress for society as a whole; I believe in man's improvement in himself. Those who insist on reading in me the intention to consider man as a finished creation are strangely mistaken. *Seraphita*, the doctrine in action of the Christian Buddha, seems to me an ample answer to this rather heedless accusation.

In certain fragments of this long work I have tried to popularize the amazing facts, I may say the marvels, of electricity, which in man is metamorphosed into an incalculable force; but in what way do the phenomena of brain and nerves, which prove the existence of an undiscovered world of psychology, modify the necessary and undoubted relations of the worlds to God? In what way can they shake the Catholic dogma? Though irrefutable facts should some day place thought in the class of fluids which are discerned only by their effects while their substance evades our senses, even when aided by so many mechanical means, the result will be the same as when Christopher Columbus detected that the earth is a sphere, and Galileo demonstrated its rotation. Our future will be unchanged. The wonders of animal magnetism, with which I have been familiar since 1820; the beautiful experiments of Gall, Lavater's successor; all the men who have studied mind as opticians have studied light—two not dissimilar things—point to a conclusion in favor of the mystics, the disciples of St. John, and of those great thinkers who have established the spiritual world—the sphere in which are revealed the relations of God and man.

A sure grasp of the purport of this work will make it clear that I attach to common, daily facts, hidden or patent to the eye, to the acts of individual lives, and to their causes and principles, the importance which historians have hitherto ascribed to the events of public national life. The unknown struggle which goes on in a valley of the Indre between Mme. de Mortsauf and her passion is perhaps as great as the most famous of battles *(Le Lys dans la Vallee)*. In one the glory of the victor is at stake; in the other it is heaven. The misfortunes of the two Birotteaus, the priest and the perfumer, to me are those of mankind. La Fosseuse *(Medecin de Campagne)* and Mme. Graslin *(Cure de Village)* are almost the sum-total of woman. We all suffer thus every day. I have had to do a hundred times what Richardson did but once. Lovelace has a thousand forms, for social corruption takes the hues of the medium in which it lives. Clarissa, on the contrary, the lovely image of impassioned virtue, is drawn in lines of distracting purity. To create a variety of Virgins it needs a Raphael. In this respect, perhaps literature must yield to painting.

Still, I may be allowed to point out how many irreproachable figures—as regards their virtue—are to be found in the portions of this work already published: Pierrette Lorrain, Ursule Mirouet, Constance Birotteau, La Fosseuse, Eugenie Grandet, Marguerite Claes, Pauline de Villenoix, Madame Jules, Madame de la Chanterie, Eve Chardon, Mademoiselle d'Esgrignon, Madame Firmiani, Agathe Rouget, Renee de Maucombe; besides several figures in the middle-distance, who, though less conspicuous than these, nevertheless, offer the reader an example of domestic virtue: Joseph Lebas, Genestas, Benassis, Bonnet the cure, Minoret the doctor, Pillerault, David Sechard, the two Birotteaus, Chaperon the priest, Judge Popinot, Bourgeat, the Sauviats, the Tascherons, and many more. Do not all these solve the difficult literary problem which consists in making a virtuous person interesting?

It was no small task to depict the two or three thousand conspicuous types of a period; for this is, in fact, the number presented to us by each generation, and which the Human Comedy will require. This crowd of actors, of characters, this multitude of lives, needed a setting—if I may be pardoned the expression, a gallery. Hence the very natural division, as already known, into the Scenes of Private Life, of Provincial Life, of Parisian, Political, Military, and Country Life. Under these six heads are classified all the studies of manners which form the history of society at large, of all its *faits et gestes*, as our ancestors would have said. These six classes correspond, indeed, to familiar conceptions. Each has its own sense and meaning, and answers to an epoch in the life of man. I may repeat here, but very briefly, what was written by Felix Davin—a young genius snatched from literature by an early death. After being informed of my plan, he said that the Scenes of Private Life represented childhood and youth and their errors, as the Scenes of Provincial Life represented the age of passion, scheming, self-interest, and ambition. Then the Scenes of Parisian Life give a picture of the tastes and vice and unbridled powers which conduce to the habits peculiar to great cities, where the extremes of good and evil meet. Each of these divisions has its local color—Paris and the Provinces—a great social antithesis which held for me immense resources.

And not man alone, but the principal events of life, fall into classes by types. There are situations which occur in every life, typical phases, and this is one of the details I most sought after. I have tried to give an idea of the different districts of our fine country. My work has its geography, as it has its genealogy and its families, its places and things, its persons and their deeds; as it has its heraldry, its nobles and commonalty, its artisans and peasants, its politicians and dandies, its army—in short, a whole world of its own.

After describing social life in these three portions, I had to delineate certain exceptional lives, which comprehend the interests of many people, or of everybody, and are in a degree outside the general law. Hence we have Scenes of Political Life. This vast picture of society being finished and complete, was it not needful to display it in its most violent phase, beside itself, as it were, either in self-defence or for the sake of conquest? Hence the Scenes of Military Life, as yet the most incomplete portion of my work, but for which room will be allowed in this edition, that it may form part of it when done. Finally, the Scenes of Country Life are, in a way, the evening of this long day, if I may so call the social drama. In that part are to be found the purest natures, and the application of the great principles of order, politics, and morality.

Such is the foundation, full of actors, full of comedies and tragedies, on which are raised the Philosophical Studies—the second part of my work, in which the social instrument of all these effects is displayed, and the ravages of the mind are painted, feeling after feeling; the first of the series, *The Magic Skin*, to some extent forms a link between the Philosophical Studies and Studies of Manners, by a work of almost Oriental fancy, in which life itself is shown in a mortal struggle with the very element of all passion.

Besides these, there will be a series of Analytical Studies, of which I will say nothing, for one only is published as yet—The Physiology of Marriage.

In the course of time I purpose writing two more works of this class. First the Pathology of Social Life, then an Anatomy of Educational Bodies, and a Monograph on Virtue.

In looking forward to what remains to be done, my readers will perhaps echo what my publishers say, "Please God to spare you!" I only ask to be less tormented by men and things than I have hitherto been since I began this terrific labor. I have had this in my favor, and I thank God for it, that the talents of the time, the finest characters and the truest friends, as noble in their private lives as the former are in public life, have wrung my hand and said, Courage!

And why should I not confess that this friendship, and the testimony here and there of persons unknown to me, have upheld me in my career, both against myself and against unjust attacks; against the calumny which has often persecuted me, against discouragement, and against the too eager hopefulness whose utterances are misinterpreted as those of overwhelming conceit? I had resolved to display stolid stoicism in the face of abuse and insults; but on two occasions base slanders have necessitated a reply. Though the advocates of forgiveness of injuries may regret that I should have displayed my skill in literary fence, there are many Christians who are of opinion that we live in times when it is as well to show sometimes that silence springs from generosity.

The vastness of a plan which includes both a history and a criticism of society, an analysis of its evils, and a discussion of its principles, authorizes me, I think, in giving to my work the title under which it now appears—*The Human Comedy*. Is this too ambitious? Is it not exact? That, when it is complete, the public must pronounce.

PARIS, July 1842

MELMOTH RECONCILED

Translated by
Ellen Marriage

To Monsieur le General Baron de Pommereul, a token of the friendship between our fathers, which survives in their sons.

DE BALZAC.

There is a special variety of human nature obtained in the Social Kingdom by a process analogous to that of the gardener's craft in the Vegetable Kingdom, to wit, by the forcing-house—a species of hybrid which can be raised neither from seed nor from slips. This product is known as the Cashier, an anthropomorphous growth, watered by religious doctrine, trained up in fear of the guillotine, pruned by vice, to flourish on a third floor with an estimable wife by his side and an uninteresting family. The number of cashiers in Paris must always be a problem for the physiologist. Has any one as yet been able to state correctly the terms of the proportion sum wherein the cashier figures as the unknown x? Where will you find the man who shall live with wealth, like a cat with a caged mouse? This man, for further qualification, shall be capable of sitting boxed in behind an iron grating for seven or eight hours a day during seven-eighths of the year, perched upon a cane-seated chair in a space as narrow as a lieutenant's cabin on board a man-of-war. Such a man must be able to defy anchylosis of the knee and thigh joints; he must have a soul above meanness, in order to live meanly; must lose all relish for money by dint of handling it. Demand this peculiar specimen of any creed, educational system, school, or institution you please, and select Paris, that city of fiery ordeals and branch establishment of hell, as the soil in which to plant the said cashier. So be it. Creeds, schools, institutions and moral systems, all human rules and regulations, great and small, will, one after another, present much the same face that an intimate friend turns upon you when you ask him to lend you a thousand francs. With a dolorous dropping of the jaw, they indicate the guillotine, much as your friend aforesaid will furnish you with the address of the money-lender, pointing you to one of the hundred gates by which a man comes to the last refuge of the destitute.

Yet nature has her freaks in the making of a man's mind; she indulges herself and makes a few honest folk now and again, and now and then a cashier.

Wherefore, that race of corsairs whom we dignify with the title of bankers, the gentry who take out a license for which they pay a thousand crowns, as the privateer takes out his letters of marque, hold these rare products of the incubations of virtue in such esteem that they confine them in cages in their counting-houses, much as governments procure and maintain specimens of strange beasts at their own charges.

If the cashier is possessed of an imagination or of a fervid temperament; if, as will sometimes happen to the most complete cashier, he loves his wife, and that wife grows tired of her lot, has ambitions, or merely some vanity in her composition, the cashier is undone. Search the chronicles of the counting-house. You will not find a single instance of a cashier attaining *a position*, as it is called. They are sent to the hulks; they go to foreign parts; they vegetate on a second floor in the Rue Saint-Louis among the market gardens of the Marais. Some day, when the cashiers of Paris come to a sense of their real value, a cashier will be hardly obtainable for money. Still, certain it is that there are people who are fit for nothing but to be cashiers, just as the bent of a certain order of mind inevitably makes for rascality. But, oh marvel of our civilization! Society rewards virtue with an income of a hundred louis in old age, a dwelling on a second floor, bread sufficient, occasional new bandana handkerchiefs, an elderly wife and her offspring.

So much for virtue. But for the opposite course, a little boldness, a faculty for keeping on the windward side of the law, as Turenne outflanked Montecuculi, and Society will sanction the theft of millions, shower ribbons upon the thief, cram him with honors, and smother him with consideration.

Government, moreover, works harmoniously with this profoundly illogical reasoner—Society. Government levies a conscription on the young intelligence of the kingdom at the age of seventeen or eighteen, a conscription of precocious brain-work before it is sent up to be submitted to a process of selection. Nurserymen sort and select seeds in much the same way. To this process the Government brings professional appraisers of talent, men who can assay brains as experts assay gold at the Mint. Five hundred such heads, set afire with hope, are sent up annually by the most progressive portion of the population; and of these the Government takes one-third, puts them in sacks called the Ecoles, and shakes them up together for three years. Though every one of these young plants represents vast productive power, they are made, as one may say, into cashiers. They receive appointments; the rank and file of engineers is made up of them; they are employed as captains of artillery; there is no (subaltern) grade to which they may not aspire. Finally, when these men, the pick of the youth of the nation, fattened on mathematics and stuffed with knowledge, have attained the age of fifty years, they have their reward, and receive as the price of their services the third-floor lodging, the wife and family, and all the comforts that sweeten life for mediocrity. If from among this race of dupes there should escape some five or six men of genius who climb the highest heights, is it not miraculous?

This is an exact statement of the relations between Talent and Probity on the one hand and Government and Society on the other, in an age that considers itself to be progressive. Without this prefatory explanation a recent occurrence in Paris would seem improbable; but preceded by this summing up of the situation, it will perhaps receive some thoughtful attention from minds capable of recognizing the real plague-spots of our civilization, a civilization which since 1815 as been moved by the spirit of gain rather than by principles of honor.

About five o'clock, on a dull autumn afternoon, the cashier of one of the largest banks in Paris was still at his desk, working by the light of a lamp that had been lit for some time. In accordance with the use and wont of commerce, the counting-house was in the darkest corner of the low-ceiled and far from spacious mezzanine floor, and at the very end of a passage lighted only by borrowed lights. The office doors along this corridor, each with its label, gave the place the look of a bath-house. At four o'clock the stolid porter had proclaimed, according to his orders, "The bank is closed." And by this time the departments were deserted, wives of the partners in the firm were expecting their lovers; the two bankers dining with their mistresses. Everything was in order.

The place where the strong boxes had been bedded in sheet-iron was just behind the little sanctum, where the cashier was busy. Doubtless he was balancing his books. The open front gave a glimpse of a safe of hammered iron, so enormously heavy (thanks to the science of the modern inventor) that burglars could not carry it away. The door only opened at the pleasure of those who knew its password. The letter-lock was a warden who kept its own secret and could not be bribed; the mysterious word was an ingenious realization of the "Open sesame!" in the *Arabian Nights*. But even this was as nothing. A man might discover the password; but unless he knew the lock's final secret, the *ultima ratio* of this gold-guarding dragon of mechanical science, it discharged a blunderbuss at his head.

The door of the room, the walls of the room, the shutters of the windows in the room, the whole place, in fact, was lined with sheet-iron a third of an inch in thickness, concealed behind the thin wooden paneling. The shutters had been closed, the door had been shut. If ever man could feel confident that he was absolutely alone, and that there was no remote possibility of being watched by prying eyes, that man was the cashier of the house of Nucingen and Company, in the Rue Saint-Lazare.

Accordingly the deepest silence prevailed in that iron cave. The fire had died out in the stove, but the room was full of that tepid warmth which produces the dull heavy-headedness and nauseous queasiness of a morning after an orgy. The stove is a mesmerist that plays no small part in the reduction of bank clerks and porters to a state of idiocy.

A room with a stove in it is a retort in which the power of strong men is evaporated, where their vitality is exhausted, and their wills enfeebled. Government offices are part of a great scheme for the manufacture of the mediocrity necessary for the maintenance of a Feudal System on a pecuniary basis—and money is the foundation of the Social Contract. (See *Les Employes*.) The mephitic vapors in the atmosphere of a crowded room contribute in no small degree to bring about a gradual deterioration of intelligences, the brain that gives off the largest quantity of nitrogen asphyxiates the others, in the long run.

The cashier was a man of five-and-forty or thereabouts. As he sat at the table, the light from a moderator lamp shining full on his bald head and glistening fringe of iron-gray hair that surrounded it—this baldness and the round outlines of his face made his head look very like a ball. His complexion was brick-red, a few wrinkles had gathered about his eyes, but he had the smooth, plump hands of a stout man. His blue cloth coat, a little rubbed and worn, and the creases and shininess of his trousers, traces of hard wear that the clothes-brush fails to remove, would impress a superficial observer with the idea that here was a thrifty and upright human being, sufficient of the philosopher or of the aristocrat to wear shabby clothes. But, unluckily, it is easy to find penny-wise people who will prove weak, wasteful, or incompetent in the capital things of life.

The cashier wore the ribbon of the Legion of Honor at his button-hole, for he had been a major of dragoons in the time of the Emperor. M. de Nucingen, who had been a contractor before he became a banker, had had reason in those days to know the honorable disposition of his cashier, who then occupied a high position. Reverses of fortune had befallen the major, and the banker out of regard for him paid him five hundred francs a month. The soldier had become a cashier in the year 1813, after his recovery from a wound received at Studzianka during the Retreat from Moscow, followed by six months of enforced idleness at Strasbourg, whither several officers had been transported by order of the Emperor, that they might receive skilled attention. This particular officer, Castanier by name, retired with the honorary grade of colonel, and a pension of two thousand four hundred francs.

In ten years' time the cashier had completely effaced the soldier, and Castanier inspired the banker with such trust in him, that he was associated in the transactions that went on in the private office behind his little counting-house. The baron himself had access to it by means of a secret staircase. There, matters of business were decided. It was the bolting-room where proposals were sifted; the privy council chamber where the reports of the money market were analyzed; circular notes issued thence; and finally, the private ledger and the journal which summarized the work of all the departments were kept there.

Castanier had gone himself to shut the door which opened on to a staircase that led to the parlor occupied by the two bankers on the first floor of their hotel. This done, he had sat down at his desk again, and for a moment he gazed at a little collection of letters of credit drawn on the firm of Watschildine of London. Then he had taken up the pen and imitated the banker's signature on each. *Nucingen* he wrote, and eyed the forged signatures critically to see which seemed the most perfect copy.

Suddenly he looked up as if a needle had pricked him. "You are not alone!" a boding voice seemed to cry in his heart; and indeed the forger saw a man standing at the little grated window of the counting-house, a man whose breathing was so noiseless that he did not seem to breathe at all. Castanier looked, and saw that the door at the end of the passage was wide open; the stranger must have entered by that way.

For the first time in his life the old soldier felt a sensation of dread that made him stare open-mouthed and wide-eyed at the man before him; and for that matter, the appearance of the apparition was sufficiently alarming even if unaccompanied by the mysterious circumstances of so sudden an entry. The rounded forehead, the harsh coloring of the long oval face, indicated quite as plainly as the cut of his clothes that the man was an Englishman, reeking of his native isles. You had only to look at the collar of his overcoat, at the voluminous cravat which smothered the crushed frills of a shirt front so white that it brought out the changeless leaden hue of an impassive face, and the thin red line of the lips that seemed made to suck the blood of corpses; and you can guess at once at the black gaiters buttoned up to the knee, and the half-puritanical costume of a wealthy Englishman dressed for a walking excursion. The intolerable glitter of the stranger's eyes produced a vivid and unpleasant impression, which was only deepened by the rigid outlines of his features. The dried-up, emaciated creature seemed to carry within him some gnawing thought that consumed him and could not be appeased.

He must have digested his food so rapidly that he could doubtless eat continually without bringing any trace of color into his face or features. A tun of Tokay *vin de succession* would not have caused any faltering in that piercing glance that read men's inmost thoughts, nor dethroned the merciless reasoning faculty that always seemed to go to the bottom of things. There was something of the fell and tranquil majesty of a tiger about him.

"I have come to cash this bill of exchange, sir," he said. Castanier felt the tones of his voice thrill through every nerve with a violent shock similar to that given by a discharge of electricity.

"The safe is closed," said Castanier.

"It is open," said the Englishman, looking round the counting-house. "Tomorrow is Sunday, and I cannot wait. The amount is for five hundred thousand francs. You have the money there, and I must have it."

"But how did you come in, sir?"

The Englishman smiled. That smile frightened Castanier. No words could have replied more fully nor more peremptorily than that scornful and imperial curl of the stranger's lips. Castanier turned away, took up fifty packets each containing ten thousand francs in bank-notes, and held them out to the stranger, receiving in exchange for them a bill accepted by the Baron de Nucingen. A sort of convulsive tremor ran through him as he saw a red gleam in the stranger's eyes when they fell on the forged signature on the letter of credit.

"It . . . it wants your signature . . ." stammered Castanier, handing back the bill.

"Hand me your pen," answered the Englishman.

Castanier handed him the pen with which he had just committed forgery. The stranger wrote *John Melmoth*, then he returned the slip of paper and the pen to the cashier. Castanier looked at the handwriting, noticing that it sloped from right to left in the Eastern fashion, and Melmoth disappeared so noiselessly that when Castanier looked up again an exclamation broke from him, partly because the man was no longer there, partly because he felt a strange painful sensation such as our imagination might take for an effect of poison.

The pen that Melmoth had handled sent the same sickening heat through him that an emetic produces. But it seemed impossible to Castanier that the Englishman should have guessed his crime. His inward qualms he attributed to the palpitation of the heart that, according to received ideas, was sure to follow at once on such a "turn" as the stranger had given him.

"The devil take it; I am very stupid. Providence is watching over me; for if that brute had come round to see my gentleman to-morrow, my goose would have been cooked!" said Castanier, and he burned the unsuccessful attempts at forgery in the stove.

He put the bill that he meant to take with him in an envelope, and helped himself to five hundred thousand francs in French and English bank-notes from the safe, which he locked. Then he put everything in order, lit a candle, blew out the lamp, took up his hat and umbrella, and went out sedately, as usual, to leave one of the two keys of the strong room with Madame de Nucingen, in the absence of her husband the Baron.

"You are in luck, M. Castanier," said the banker's wife as he entered the room; "we have a holiday on Monday; you can go into the country, or to Soizy."

"Madame, will you be so good as to tell your husband that the bill of exchange on Watschildine, which was behind time, has just been presented? The five hundred thousand francs have been paid; so I shall not come back till noon on Tuesday."

"Good-bye, monsieur; I hope you will have a pleasant time."

"The same to you, madame," replied the old dragoon as he went out. He glanced as he spoke at a young man well known in fashionable society at that time, a M. de Rastignac, who was regarded as Madame de Nucingen's lover.

"Madame," remarked this latter, "the old boy looks to me as if he meant to play you some ill turn."

"Pshaw! impossible; he is too stupid."

"Piquoizeau," said the cashier, walking into the porter's room, "what made you let anybody come up after four o'clock?"

"I have been smoking a pipe here in the doorway ever since four o'clock," said the man, "and nobody has gone into the bank. Nobody has come out either except the gentlemen—"

"Are you quite sure?"

"Yes, upon my word and honor. Stay, though, at four o'clock M. Werbrust's friend came, a young fellow from Messrs. du Tillet & Co., in the Rue Joubert."

"All right," said Castanier, and he hurried away.

The sickening sensation of heat that he had felt when he took back the pen returned in greater intensity. *"Mille diables!"* thought he, as he threaded his way along the Boulevard de Gand, "haven't I taken proper precautions? Let me think! Two clear days, Sunday and Monday, then a day of uncertainty before they begin to look for me; altogether, three days and four nights' respite. I have a couple of passports and two different disguises; is not that enough to throw the cleverest detective off the scent? On Tuesday morning I shall draw a million francs in London before the slightest suspicion has been aroused. My debts I am leaving behind for the benefit of my creditors, who will put a 'P'* on the bills, and I shall live comfortably in Italy for the rest of my days as the Conte Ferraro. [*Protested.] I was alone with him when he died, poor fellow, in the marsh of Zembin, and I shall slip into his skin . . . *Mille diables*! the woman who is to follow after me might give them a clue! Think of an old campaigner like me infatuated enough to tie myself to a petticoat tail! . . . Why take her? I must leave her behind. Yes, I could make up my mind to it; but—I know myself—I should be ass enough to go back to her. Still, nobody knows Aquilina. Shall I take her or leave her?"

"You will not take her!" cried a voice that filled Castanier with sickening dread. He turned sharply, and saw the Englishman.

"The devil is in it!" cried the cashier aloud.

Melmoth had passed his victim by this time; and if Castanier's first impulse had been to fasten a quarrel on a man who read his own thoughts, he was so much torn up by opposing feelings that the immediate result was a temporary paralysis. When he resumed his walk he fell once more into that fever of irresolution which besets those who are so carried away by passion that they are ready to commit a crime, but have not sufficient strength of character to keep it to themselves without suffering terribly in the process. So, although Castanier had made up his mind to reap the fruits of a crime which was already half executed, he hesitated to carry out his designs. For him, as for many men of mixed character in whom weakness and strength are equally blended, the least trifling consideration determines whether they shall continue to lead blameless lives or become actively criminal. In the vast masses of men enrolled in Napoleon's armies there are many who, like Castanier, possessed the purely physical courage demanded on the battlefield, yet lacked the moral courage which makes a man as great in crime as he could have been in virtue.

The letter of credit was drafted in such terms that immediately on his arrival he might draw twenty-five thousand pounds on the firm of Watschildine, the London correspondents of the house of Nucingen. The London house had already been advised of the draft about to be made upon them, he had written to them himself. He had instructed an agent (chosen at random) to take his passage in a vessel which was to leave Portsmouth with a wealthy English family on board, who were going to Italy, and the passage-money had been paid in the name of the Conte Ferraro. The smallest details of the scheme had been thought out. He had arranged matters so as to divert the search that would be made for him into Belgium and Switzerland, while he himself was at sea in the English vessel. Then, by the time that Nucingen might flatter himself that he was on the track of his late cashier, the said cashier, as the Conte Ferraro, hoped to be safe in Naples. He had determined to disfigure his face in order to disguise himself the more completely, and by means of an acid to imitate the scars of smallpox. Yet, in spite of all these precautions, which surely seemed as if they must secure him complete immunity, his conscience tormented him; he was afraid. The even and peaceful life that he had led for so long had modified the morality of the camp. His life was stainless as yet; he could not sully it without a pang. So for the last time he abandoned himself to all the influences of the better self that strenuously resisted.

"Pshaw!" he said at last, at the corner of the Boulevard and the Rue Montmartre, "I will take a cab after the play this evening and go out to Versailles. A post-chaise will be ready for me at my old quartermaster's place. He would keep my secret even if a dozen men were standing ready to shoot him down. The chances are all in my favor, so far as I see; so I shall take my little Naqui with me, and I will go."

"You will not go!" exclaimed the Englishman, and the strange tones of his voice drove all the cashier's blood back to his heart.

Melmoth stepped into a tilbury which was waiting for him, and was whirled away so quickly, that when Castanier looked up he saw his foe some hundred paces away from him, and before it even crossed his mind to cut off the man's retreat the tilbury was far on its way up the Boulevard Montmartre.

"Well, upon my word, there is something supernatural about this!" said he to himself. "If I were fool enough to believe in God, I should think that He had set Saint Michael on my tracks. Suppose that the devil and the police should let me go on as I please, so as to nab me in the nick of time? Did any one ever see the like! But there, this is folly . . ."

Castanier went along the Rue du Faubourg-Montmartre, slackening his pace as he neared the Rue Richer. There on the second floor of a block of buildings which looked out upon some gardens lived the unconscious cause of Castanier's crime—a young woman known in the quarter as Mme. de la Garde. A concise history of certain events in the cashier's past life must be given in order to explain these facts, and to give a complete presentment of the crisis when he yielded to temptation.

Mme. de la Garde said that she was a Piedmontese. No one, not even Castanier, knew her real name. She was one of those young girls, who are driven by dire misery, by inability to earn a living, or by fear of starvation, to have recourse to a trade which most of them loathe, many regard with indifference, and some few follow in obedience to the laws of their constitution. But on the brink of the gulf of prostitution in Paris, the young girl of sixteen, beautiful and pure as the Madonna, had met with Castanier. The old dragoon was too rough and homely to make his way in society, and he was tired of tramping the boulevard at night and of the kind of conquests made there by gold. For some time past he had desired to bring a certain regularity into an irregular life. He was struck by the beauty of the poor child who had drifted by chance into his arms, and his determination to rescue her from the life of the streets was half benevolent, half selfish, as some of the thoughts of the best of men are apt to be. Social conditions mingle elements of evil with the promptings of natural goodness of heart, and the mixture of motives underlying a man's intentions should be leniently judged. Castanier had just cleverness enough to be very shrewd where his own interests were concerned. So he concluded to be a philanthropist on either count, and at first made her his mistress.

"Hey! hey!" he said to himself, in his soldierly fashion. "I am an old wolf, and a sheep shall not make a fool of me. Castanier, old man, before you set up housekeeping, reconnoitre the girl's character for a bit, and see if she is a steady sort."

This irregular union gave the Piedmontese a status the most nearly approaching respectability among those which the world declines to recognize. During the first year she took the *nom de guerre* of Aquilina, one of the characters in *Venice Preserved* which she had chanced to read. She fancied that she resembled the courtesan in face and general appearance, and in a certain precocity of heart and brain of which she was conscious. When Castanier found that her life was as well regulated and virtuous as was possible for a social outlaw, he manifested a desire that they should live as husband and wife. So she took the name of Mme. de la Garde, in order to approach, as closely as Parisian usages permit, the conditions of a real marriage. As a matter of fact, many of these unfortunate girls have one fixed idea, to be looked upon as respectable middle-class women, who lead humdrum lives of faithfulness to their husbands; women who would make excellent mothers, keepers of household accounts, and menders of household linen. This longing springs from a sentiment so laudable, that society should take it into consideration. But society, incorrigible as ever, will assuredly persist in regarding the married woman as a corvette duly authorized by her flag and papers to go on her own course, while the woman who is a wife in all but name is a pirate and an outlaw for lack of a document. A day came when Mme. de la Garde would fain have signed herself "Mme. Castanier." The cashier was put out by this.

"So you do not love me well enough to marry me?" she said.

Castanier did not answer; he was absorbed by his thoughts. The poor girl resigned herself to her fate. The ex-dragoon was in despair. Naqui's heart softened towards him at the sight of his trouble; she tried to soothe him, but what could she do when she did not know what ailed him? When Naqui made up her mind to know the secret, although she never asked him a question, the cashier dolefully confessed to the existence of a Mme. Castanier. This lawful wife, a thousand times accursed, was living in a humble way in Strasbourg on a small property there; he wrote to her twice a year, and kept the secret of her existence so well, that no one suspected that he was married. The reason of this reticence? If it is familiar to many military men who may chance to be in a like predicament, it is perhaps worth while to give the story.

Your genuine trooper (if it is allowable here to employ the word which in the army signifies a man who is destined to die as a captain) is a sort of serf, a part and parcel of his regiment, an essentially simple creature, and Castanier was marked out by nature as a victim to the wiles of mothers with grown-up daughters left too long on their hands. It was at Nancy, during one of those brief intervals of repose when the Imperial armies were not on active service abroad, that Castanier was so unlucky as to pay some attention to a young lady with whom he danced at a *ridotto*, the provincial name for the entertainments often given by the military to the townsfolk, or vice versa, in garrison towns. A scheme for inveigling the gallant captain into matrimony was immediately set on foot, one of those schemes by which mothers secure accomplices in a human heart by touching all its motive springs, while they convert all their friends into fellow-conspirators. Like all people possessed by one idea, these ladies press everything into the service of their great project, slowly elaborating their toils, much as the ant-lion excavates its funnel in the sand and lies in wait at the bottom for its victim. Suppose that no one strays, after all, into that carefully constructed labyrinth? Suppose that the ant-lion dies of hunger and thirst in her pit? Such things may be, but if any heedless creature once enters in, it never comes out. All the wires which could be pulled to induce action on the captain's part were tried; appeals were made to the secret interested motives that always come into play in such cases; they worked on Castanier's hopes and on the weaknesses and vanity of human nature. Unluckily, he had praised the daughter to her mother when he brought her back after a waltz, a little chat followed, and then an invitation in the most natural way in the world. Once introduced into the house, the dragoon was dazzled by the hospitality of a family who appeared to conceal their real wealth beneath a show of careful economy. He was skilfully flattered on all sides, and every one extolled for his benefit the various treasures there displayed. A neatly timed dinner, served on plate lent by an uncle, the attention shown to him by the only daughter of the house, the gossip of the town, a well-to-do sub-lieutenant who seemed likely to cut the ground from under his feet—all the innumerable snares, in short, of the provincial ant-lion were set for him, and to such good purpose, that Castanier said five years later, "To this day I do not know how it came about!"

The dragoon received fifteen thousand francs with the lady, who after two years of marriage, became the ugliest and consequently the most peevish woman on earth. Luckily they had no children. The fair complexion (maintained by a Spartan regimen), the fresh, bright color in her face, which spoke of an engaging modesty, became overspread with blotches and pimples; her figure, which had seemed so straight, grew crooked, the angel became a suspicious and shrewish creature who drove Castanier frantic. Then the fortune took to itself wings. At length the dragoon, no longer recognizing the woman whom he had wedded, left her to live on a little property at Strasbourg, until the time when it should please God to remove her to adorn Paradise. She was one of those virtuous women who, for want of other occupation, would weary the life out of an angel with complainings, who pray till (if their prayers are heard in heaven) they must exhaust the patience of the Almighty, and say everything that is bad of their husbands in dovelike murmurs over a game of boston with their neighbors. When Aquilina learned all these troubles she clung still more affectionately to Castanier, and made him so happy, varying with woman's ingenuity the pleasures with which she filled his life, that all unwittingly she was the cause of the cashier's downfall.

Like many women who seem by nature destined to sound all the depths of love, Mme. de la Garde was disinterested. She asked neither for gold nor for jewelry, gave no thought to the future, lived entirely for the present and for the pleasures of the present. She accepted expensive ornaments and dresses, the carriage so eagerly coveted by women of her class, as one harmony the more in the picture of life. There was absolutely no vanity in her desire not to appear at a better advantage but to look the fairer, and moreover, no woman could live without luxuries more cheerfully. When a man of generous nature (and military men are mostly of this stamp) meets with such a woman, he feels a sort of exasperation at finding himself her debtor in generosity. He feels that he could stop a mail coach to obtain money for her if he has not sufficient for her whims. He will commit a crime if so he may be great and noble in the eyes of some woman or of his special public; such is the nature of the man. Such a lover is like a gambler who would be dishonored in his own eyes if he did not repay the sum he borrowed from a waiter in a gaming-house; but will shrink from no crime, will leave his wife and children without a penny, and rob and murder, if so he may come to the gaming-table with a full purse, and his honor remain untarnished among the frequenters of that fatal abode. So it was with Castanier.

He had begun by installing Aquiline is a modest fourth-floor dwelling, the furniture being of the simplest kind. But when he saw the girl's beauty and great qualities, when he had known inexpressible and unlooked-for happiness with her, he began to dote upon her; and longed to adorn his idol. Then Aquilina's toilette was so comically out of keeping with her poor abode, that for both their sakes it was clearly incumbent on him to move. The change swallowed up almost all Castanier's savings, for he furnished his domestic paradise with all the prodigality that is lavished on a kept mistress. A pretty woman must have everything pretty about her; the unity of charm in the woman and her surroundings singles her out from among her sex. This sentiment of homogeneity indeed, though it has frequently escaped the attention of observers, is instinctive in human nature; and the same prompting leads elderly spinsters to surround themselves with dreary relics of the past. But the lovely Piedmontese must have the newest and latest fashions, and all that was daintiest and prettiest in stuffs for hangings, in silks or jewelry, in fine china and other brittle and fragile wares. She asked for nothing; but when she was called upon to make a choice, when Castanier asked her, "Which do you like?" she would answer, "Why, this is the nicest!" Love never counts the cost, and Castanier therefore always took the "nicest."

When once the standard had been set up, there was nothing for it but everything in the household must be in conformity, from the linen, plate, and crystal through a thousand and one items of expenditure down to the pots and pans in the kitchen. Castanier had meant to "do things simply," as the saying goes, but he gradually found himself more and more in debt. One expense entailed another. The clock called for candle sconces. Fires must be lighted in the ornamental grates, but the curtains and hangings were too fresh and delicate to be soiled by smuts, so they must be replaced by patent and elaborate fireplaces, warranted to give out no smoke, recent inventions of the people who are so clever at drawing up a prospectus. Then Aquilina found it so nice to run about barefooted on the carpet in her room, that Castanier must have soft carpets laid everywhere for the pleasure of playing with Naqui. A bathroom, too, was built for her, everything to the end that she might be more comfortable.

Shopkeepers, workmen, and manufacturers in Paris have a mysterious knack of enlarging a hole in a man's purse. They cannot give the price of anything upon inquiry; and as the paroxysm of longing cannot abide delay, orders are given by the feeble light of an approximate estimate of cost. The same people never send in the bills at once, but ply the purchaser with furniture till his head spins. Everything is so pretty, so charming; and every one is satisfied.

A few months later the obliging furniture dealers are metamorphosed, and reappear in the shape of alarming totals on invoices that fill the soul with their horrid clamor; they are in urgent want of the money; they are, as you may say on the brink of bankruptcy, their tears flow, it is heartrending to hear them! And then—the gulf yawns, and gives up serried columns of figures marching four deep, when as a matter of fact they should have issued innocently three by three.

Before Castanier had any idea of how much he had spent, he had arranged for Aquilina to have a carriage from a livery stable when she went out, instead of a cab. Castanier was a gourmand; he engaged an excellent cook; and Aquilina, to please him, had herself made the purchases of early fruit and vegetables, rare delicacies, and exquisite wines. But, as Aquilina had nothing of her own, these gifts of hers, so precious by reason of the thought and tact and graciousness that prompted them, were no less a drain upon Castanier's purse; he did not like his Naqui to be without money, and Naqui could not keep money in her pocket. So the table was a heavy item of expenditure for a man with Castanier's income. The ex-dragoon was compelled to resort to various shifts for obtaining money, for he could not bring himself to renounce this delightful life. He loved the woman too well to cross the freaks of the mistress. He was one of those men who, through self-love or through weakness of character, can refuse nothing to a woman; false shame overpowers them, and they rather face ruin than make the admissions: "I cannot—" "My means will not permit—" "I cannot afford—"

When, therefore, Castanier saw that if he meant to emerge from the abyss of debt into which he had plunged, he must part with Aquilina and live upon bread and water, he was so unable to do without her or to change his habits of life, that daily he put off his plans of reform until the morrow. The debts were pressing, and he began by borrowing money. His position and previous character inspired confidence, and of this he took advantage to devise a system of borrowing money as he required it. Then, as the total amount of debt rapidly increased, he had recourse to those commercial inventions known as accommodation bills. This form of bill does not represent goods or other value received, and the first endorser pays the amount named for the obliging person who accepts it. This species of fraud is tolerated because it is impossible to detect it, and, moreover, it is an imaginary fraud which only becomes real if payment is ultimately refused.

When at length it was evidently impossible to borrow any longer, whether because the amount of the debt was now so greatly increased, or because Castanier was unable to pay the large amount of interest on the aforesaid sums of money, the cashier saw bankruptcy before him. On making this discovery, he decided for a fraudulent bankruptcy rather than an ordinary failure, and preferred a crime to a misdemeanor. He determined, after the fashion of the celebrated cashier of the Royal Treasury, to abuse the trust deservedly won, and to increase the number of his creditors by making a final loan of the sum sufficient to keep him in comfort in a foreign country for the rest of his days. All this, as has been seen, he had prepared to do.

Aquilina knew nothing of the irksome cares of this life; she enjoyed her existence, as many a woman does, making no inquiry as to where the money came from, even as sundry other folk will eat their buttered rolls untroubled by any restless spirit of curiosity as to the culture and growth of wheat; but as the labor and miscalculations of agriculture lie on the other side of the baker's oven, so beneath the unappreciated luxury of many a Parisian household lie intolerable anxieties and exorbitant toil.

While Castanier was enduring the torture of the strain, and his thoughts were full of the deed that should change his whole life, Aquilina was lying luxuriously back in a great armchair by the fireside, beguiling the time by chatting with her waiting-maid. As frequently happens in such cases the maid had become the mistress' confidant, Jenny having first assured herself that her mistress' ascendency over Castanier was complete.

"What are we to do this evening? Leon seems determined to come," Mme. de la Garde was saying, as she read a passionate epistle indited upon a faint gray notepaper.

"Here is the master!" said Jenny.

Castanier came in. Aquilina, nowise disconcerted, crumpled up the letter, took it with the tongs, and held it in the flames.

"So that is what you do with your love-letters, is it?" asked Castanier.

"Oh goodness, yes," said Aquilina; "is not the best way of keeping them safe? Besides, fire should go to fire, as water makes for the river."

"You are talking as if it were a real love-letter, Naqui—"

"Well, am I not handsome enough to receive them?" she said, holding up her forehead for a kiss. There was a carelessness in her manner that would have told any man less blind than Castanier that it was only a piece of conjugal duty, as it were, to give this joy to the cashier, but use and wont had brought Castanier to the point where clear-sightedness is no longer possible for love.

"I have taken a box at the Gymnase this evening," he said; "let us have dinner early, and then we need not dine in a hurry."

"Go and take Jenny. I am tired of plays. I do not know what is the matter with me this evening; I would rather stay here by the fire."

"Come, all the same though, Naqui; I shall not be here to bore you much longer. Yes, Quiqui, I am going to start to-night, and it will be some time before I come back again. I am leaving everything in your charge. Will you keep your heart for me too?"

"Neither my heart nor anything else," she said; "but when you come back again, Naqui will still be Naqui for you."

"Well, this is frankness. So you would not follow me?"

"No."

"Why not?"

"Eh! why, how can I leave the lover who writes me such sweet little notes?" she asked, pointing to the blackened scrap of paper with a mocking smile.

"Is there any truth in it?" asked Castanier. "Have you really a lover?"

"Really!" cried Aquilina; "and have you never given it a serious thought, dear? To begin with, you are fifty years old. Then you have just the sort of face to put on a fruit stall; if the woman tried to see you for a pumpkin, no one would contradict her. You puff and blow like a seal when you come upstairs; your paunch rises and falls like a diamond on a woman's forehead! It is pretty plain that you served in the dragoons; you are a very ugly-looking old man. Fiddle-de-dee. If you have any mind to keep my respect, I recommend you not to add imbecility to these qualities by imagining that such a girl as I am will be content with your asthmatic love, and not look for youth and good looks and pleasure by way of a variety—"

"Aquilina! you are laughing, of course?"

"Oh, very well; and are you not laughing too? Do you take me for a fool, telling me that you are going away? 'I am going to start to-night!'" she said, mimicking his tones. "Stuff and nonsense! Would you talk like that if you were really going from your Naqui? You would cry, like the booby that you are!"

"After all, if I go, will you follow?" he asked.

"Tell me first whether this journey of yours is a bad joke or not."

"Yes, seriously, I am going."

"Well, then, seriously, I shall stay. A pleasant journey to you, my boy! I will wait till you come back. I would sooner take leave of life than take leave of my dear, cozy Paris—"

"Will you not come to Italy, to Naples, and lead a pleasant life there—a delicious, luxurious life, with this stout old fogy of yours, who puffs and blows like a seal?"

"No."

"Ungrateful girl!"

"Ungrateful?" she cried, rising to her feet. "I might leave this house this moment and take nothing out of it but myself. I shall have given you all the treasures a young girl can give, and something that not every drop in your veins and mine can ever give me back. If, by any means whatever, by selling my hopes of eternity, for instance, I could recover my past self, body and soul (for I have, perhaps, redeemed my soul), and be pure as a lily for my lover, I would not hesitate a moment! What sort of devotion has rewarded mine? You have housed and fed me, just as you give a dog food and a kennel because he is a protection to the house, and he may take kicks when we are out of humor, and lick our hands as soon as we are pleased to call him. And which of us two will have been the more generous?"

"Oh! dear child, do you not see that I am joking?" returned Castanier. "I am going on a short journey; I shall not be away for very long. But come with me to the Gymnase; I shall start just before midnight, after I have had time to say good-bye to you."

"Poor pet! so you are really going, are you?" she said. She put her arms round his neck, and drew down his head against her bodice.

"You are smothering me!" cried Castanier, with his face buried in Aquilina's breast. That damsel turned to say in Jenny's ear, "Go to Leon, and tell him not to come till one o'clock. If you do not find him, and he comes here during the leave-taking, keep him in your room.—Well," she went on, setting free Castanier, and giving a tweak to the tip of his nose, "never mind, handsomest of seals that you are. I will go to the theatre with you this evening? But all in good time; let us have dinner! There is a nice little dinner for you—just what you like."

"It is very hard to part from such a woman as you!" exclaimed Castanier.

"Very well then, why do you go?" asked she.

"Ah! why? why? If I were to begin to begin to explain the reasons why, I must tell you things that would prove to you that I love you almost to madness. Ah! if you have sacrificed your honor for me, I have sold mine for you; we are quits. Is that love?"

"What is all this about?" said she. "Come, now, promise me that if I had a lover you would still love me as a father; that would be love! Come, now, promise it at once, and give us your fist upon it."

"I should kill you," and Castanier smiled as he spoke.

They sat down to the dinner table, and went thence to the Gymnase. When the first part of the performance was over, it occurred to Castanier to show himself to some of his acquaintances in the house, so as to turn away any suspicion of his departure. He left Mme. de la Garde in the corner box where she was seated, according to her modest wont, and went to walk up and down in the lobby. He had not gone many paces before he saw the Englishman, and with a sudden return of the sickening sensation of heat that once before had vibrated through him, and of the terror that he had felt already, he stood face to face with Melmoth.

"Forger!"

At the word, Castanier glanced round at the people who were moving about them. He fancied that he could see astonishment and curiosity in their eyes, and wishing to be rid of this Englishman at once, he raised his hand to strike him—and felt his arm paralyzed by some invisible power that sapped his strength and nailed him to the spot. He allowed the stranger to take him by the arm, and they walked together to the green-room like two friends.

"Who is strong enough to resist me?" said the Englishman, addressing him. "Do you not know that everything here on earth must obey me, that it is in my power to do everything? I read men's thoughts, I see the future, and I know the past. I am here, and I can be elsewhere also. Time and space and distance are nothing to me. The whole world is at my beck and call. I have the power of continual enjoyment and of giving joy. I can see through walls, discover hidden treasures, and fill my hands with them. Palaces arise at my nod, and my architect makes no mistakes. I can make all lands break forth into blossom, heap up their gold and precious stones, and surround myself with fair women and ever new faces; everything is yielded up to my will. I could gamble on the Stock Exchange, and my speculations would be infallible; but a man who can find the hoards that misers have hidden in the earth need not trouble himself about stocks. Feel the strength of the hand that grasps you; poor wretch, doomed to shame! Try to bend the arm of iron! try to soften the adamantine heart! Fly from me if you dare! You would hear my voice in the depths of the caves that lie under the Seine; you might hide in the Catacombs, but would you not see me there? My voice could be heard through the sound of thunder, my eyes shine as brightly as the sun, for I am the peer of Lucifer!"

Castanier heard the terrible words, and felt no protest nor contradiction within himself. He walked side by side with the Englishman, and had no power to leave him.

"You are mine; you have just committed a crime. I have found at last the mate whom I have sought. Have you a mind to learn your destiny? Aha! you came here to see a play, and you shall see a play—nay, two. Come. Present me to Mme. de la Garde as one of your best friends. Am I not your last hope of escape?"

Castanier, followed by the stranger, returned to his box; and in accordance with the order he had just received, he hastened to introduce Melmoth to Mme. de la Garde. Aquilina seemed to be not in the least surprised. The Englishman declined to take a seat in front, and Castanier was once more beside his mistress; the man's slightest wish must be obeyed. The last piece was about to begin, for, at that time, small theatres gave only three pieces. One of the actors had made the Gymnase the fashion, and that evening Perlet (the actor in question) was to play in a vaudeville called *Le Comedien d'Etampes*, in which he filled four different parts.

When the curtain rose, the stranger stretched out his hand over the crowded house. Castanier's cry of terror died away, for the walls of his throat seemed glued together as Melmoth pointed to the stage, and the cashier knew that the play had been changed at the Englishman's desire.

He saw the strong-room at the bank; he saw the Baron de Nucingen in conference with a police-officer from the Prefecture, who was informing him of Castanier's conduct, explaining that the cashier had absconded with money taken from the safe, giving the history of the forged signature. The information was put in writing; the document signed and duly despatched to the Public Prosecutor.

"Are we in time, do you think?" asked Nucingen.

"Yes," said the agent of police; "he is at the Gymnase, and has no suspicion of anything."

Castanier fidgeted on his chair, and made as if he would leave the theatre, but Melmoth's hand lay on his shoulder, and he was obliged to sit and watch; the hideous power of the man produced an effect like that of nightmare, and he could not move a limb. Nay, the man himself was the nightmare; his presence weighed heavily on his victim like a poisoned atmosphere. When the wretched cashier turned to implore the Englishman's mercy, he met those blazing eyes that discharged electric currents, which pierced through him and transfixed him like darts of steel.

"What have I done to you?" he said, in his prostrate helplessness, and he breathed hard like a stag at the water's edge. "What do you want of me?"

"Look!" cried Melmoth.

Castanier looked at the stage. The scene had been changed. The play seemed to be over, and Castanier beheld himself stepping from the carriage with Aquilina; but as he entered the courtyard of the house on the Rue Richer, the scene again was suddenly changed, and he saw his own house. Jenny was chatting by the fire in her mistress' room with a subaltern officer of a line regiment then stationed at Paris.

"He is going, is he?" said the sergeant, who seemed to belong to a family in easy circumstances; "I can be happy at my ease! I love Aquilina too well to allow her to belong to that old toad! I, myself, am going to marry Mme. de la Garde!" cried the sergeant.

"Old toad!" Castanier murmured piteously.

"Here come the master and mistress; hide yourself! Stay, get in here Monsieur Leon," said Jenny. "The master won't stay here for very long."

Castanier watched the sergeant hide himself among Aquilina's gowns in her dressing-room. Almost immediately he himself appeared upon the scene, and took leave of his mistress, who made fun of him in "asides" to Jenny, while she uttered the sweetest and tenderest words in his ears. She wept with one side of her face, and laughed with the other. The audience called for an encore.

"Accursed creature!" cried Castanier from his box.

Aquilina was laughing till the tears came into her eyes.

"Goodness!" she cried, "how funny Perlet is as the Englishwoman! . . . Why don't you laugh? Every one else in the house is laughing. Laugh, dear!" she said to Castanier.

Melmoth burst out laughing, and the unhappy cashier shuddered. The Englishman's laughter wrung his heart and tortured his brain; it was as if a surgeon had bored his skull with a red-hot iron.

"Laughing! are they laughing!" stammered Castanier.

He did not see the prim English lady whom Perlet was acting with such ludicrous effect, nor hear the English-French that had filled the house with roars of laughter; instead of all this, he beheld himself hurrying from the Rue Richer, hailing a cab on the Boulevard, bargaining with the man to take him to Versailles. Then once more the scene changed. He recognized the sorry inn at the corner of the Rue de l'Orangerie and the Rue des Recollets, which was kept by his old quartermaster. It was two o'clock in the morning, the most perfect stillness prevailed, no one was there to watch his movements. The post-horses were put into the carriage (it came from a house in the Avenue de Paris in which an Englishman lived, and had been ordered in the foreigner's name to avoid raising suspicion). Castanier saw that he had his bills and his passports, stepped into the carriage, and set out. But at the barrier he saw two gendarmes lying in wait for the carriage. A cry of horror burst from him but Melmoth gave him a glance, and again the sound died in his throat.

"Keep your eyes on the stage, and be quiet!" said the Englishman.

In another moment Castanier saw himself flung into prison at the Conciergerie; and in the fifth act of the drama, entitled *The Cashier*, he saw himself, in three months' time, condemned to twenty years of penal servitude. Again a cry broke from him. He was exposed upon the Place du Palais-de-Justice, and the executioner branded him with a red-hot iron. Then came the last scene of all; among some sixty convicts in the prison yard of the Bicetre, he was awaiting his turn to have the irons riveted on his limbs.

"Dear me! I cannot laugh any more! . . ." said Aquilina. "You are very solemn, dear boy; what can be the matter? The gentleman has gone."

"A word with you, Castanier," said Melmoth when the piece was at an end, and the attendant was fastening Mme. de la Garde's cloak.

The corridor was crowded, and escape impossible.

"Very well, what is it?"

"No human power can hinder you from taking Aquilina home, and going next to Versailles, there to be arrested."

"How so?"

"Because you are in a hand that will never relax its grasp," returned the Englishman.

Castanier longed for the power to utter some word that should blot him out from among living men and hide him in the lowest depths of hell.

"Suppose that the Devil were to make a bid for your soul, would you not give it to him now in exchange for the power of God? One single word, and those five hundred thousand francs shall be back in the Baron de Nucingen's safe; then you can tear up the letter of credit, and all traces of your crime will be obliterated. Moreover, you would have gold in torrents. You hardly believe in anything perhaps? Well, if all this comes to pass, you will believe at least in the Devil."

"If it were only possible!" said Castanier joyfully.

"The man who can do it all gives you his word that it is possible," answered the Englishman.

Melmoth, Castanier, and Mme. de la Garde were standing out in the Boulevard when Melmoth raised his arm. A drizzling rain was falling, the streets were muddy, the air was close, there was thick darkness overhead; but in a moment, as the arm was outstretched, Paris was filled with sunlight; it was high noon on a bright July day. The trees were covered with leaves; a double stream of joyous holiday makers strolled beneath them. Sellers of liquorice water shouted their cool drinks. Splendid carriages rolled past along the streets. A cry of terror broke from the cashier, and at that cry rain and darkness once more settled down upon the Boulevard.

Mme. de la Garde had stepped into the carriage. "Do be quick, dear!" she cried; "either come in or stay out. Really you are as dull as ditch-water this evening—"

"What must I do?" Castanier asked of Melmoth.

"Would you like to take my place?" inquired the Englishman.

"Yes."

"Very well, then; I will be at your house in a few moments."

"By the by, Castanier, you are rather off your balance," Aquilina remarked. "There is some mischief brewing: you were quite melancholy and thoughtful all through the play. Do you want anything that I can give you, dear? Tell me."

"I am waiting till we are at home to know whether you love me."

"You need not wait till then," she said, throwing her arms round his neck. "There!" she said, as she embraced him, passionately to all appearance, and plied him with the coaxing caresses that are part of the business of such a life as hers, like stage action for an actress.

"Where is the music?" asked Castanier.

"What next? Only think of your hearing music now!"

"Heavenly music!" he went on. "The sounds seem to come from above."

"What? You have always refused to give me a box at the Italiens because you could not abide music, and are you turning music-mad at this time of day? Mad—that you are! The music is inside your own noddle, old addle-pate!" she went on, as she took his head in her hands and rocked it to and fro on her shoulder. "Tell me now, old man; isn't it the creaking of the wheels that sings in your ears?"

"Just listen, Naqui! If the angels make music for God Almighty, it must be such music as this that I am drinking in at every pore, rather than hearing. I do no know how to tell you about it; it is as sweet as honey-water!"

"Why, of course, they have music in heaven, for the angels in all the pictures have harps in their hands. He is mad, upon my word!" she said to herself, as she saw Castanier's attitude; he looked like an opium-eater in a blissful trance.

They reached the house. Castanier, absorbed by the thought of all that he had just heard and seen, knew not whether to believe it or not; he was like a drunken man, and utterly unable to think connectedly. He came to himself in Aquilina's room, whither he had been supported by the united efforts of his mistress, the porter, and Jenny; for he had fainted as he stepped from the carriage.

"*He* will be here directly! Oh, my friends, my friends," he cried, and he flung himself despairingly into the depths of a low chair beside the fire.

Jenny heard the bell as he spoke, and admitted the Englishman. She announced that "a gentleman had come who had made an appointment with the master," when Melmoth suddenly appeared, and deep silence followed. He looked at the porter—the porter went; he looked at Jenny—and Jenny went likewise.

"Madame," said Melmoth, turning to Aquilina, "with your permission, we will conclude a piece of urgent business."

He took Castanier's hand, and Castanier rose, and the two men went into the drawing-room. There was no light in the room, but Melmoth's eyes lit up the thickest darkness. The gaze of those strange eyes had left Aquilina like one spellbound; she was helpless, unable to take any thought for her lover; moreover, she believed him to be safe in Jenny's room, whereas their early return had taken the waiting-woman by surprise, and she had hidden the officer in the dressing-room. It had all happened exactly as in the drama that Melmoth had displayed for his victim. Presently the house-door was slammed violently, and Castanier reappeared.

"What ails you?" cried the horror-struck Aquilina.

There was a change in the cashier's appearance. A strange pallor overspread his once rubicund countenance; it wore the peculiarly sinister and stony look of the mysterious visitor. The sullen glare of his eyes was intolerable, the fierce light in them seemed to scorch. The man who had looked so good-humored and good-natured had suddenly grown tyrannical and proud. The courtesan thought that Castanier had grown thinner; there was a terrible majesty in his brow; it was as if a dragon breathed forth a malignant influence that weighed upon the others like a close, heavy atmosphere. For a moment Aquilina knew not what to do.

"What has passed between you and that diabolical-looking man in those few minutes?" she asked at length.

"I have sold my soul to him. I feel it; I am no longer the same. He has taken my *self*, and given me his soul in exchange."

"What?"

"You would not understand it at all . . . Ah! he was right," Castanier went on, "the fiend was right! I see everything and know all things.—You have been deceiving me!"

Aquilina turned cold with terror. Castanier lighted a candle and went into the dressing-room. The unhappy girl followed him with dazed bewilderment, and great was her astonishment when Castanier drew the dresses that hung there aside and disclosed the sergeant.

"Come out, my boy," said the cashier; and, taking Leon by a button of his overcoat, he drew the officer into his room.

The Piedmontese, haggard and desperate, had flung herself into her easy-chair. Castanier seated himself on a sofa by the fire, and left Aquilina's lover in a standing position.

"You have been in the army," said Leon; "I am ready to give you satisfaction."

"You are a fool," said Castanier drily. "I have no occasion to fight. I could kill you by a look if I had any mind to do it. I will tell you what it is, youngster; why should I kill you? I can see a red line round your neck—the guillotine is waiting for you. Yes, you will end in the Place de Greve. You are the headsman's property! there is no escape for you. You belong to a vendita, of the Carbonari. You are plotting against the Government."

"You did not tell me that," cried the Piedmontese, turning to Leon.

"So you do not know that the Minister decided this morning to put down your Society?" the cashier continued. "The Procureur-General has a list of your names. You have been betrayed. They are busy drawing up the indictment at this moment."

"Then was it you who betrayed him?" cried Aquilina, and with a hoarse sound in her throat like the growl of a tigress she rose to her feet; she seemed as if she would tear Castanier in pieces.

"You know me too well to believe it," Castanier retorted. Aquilina was benumbed by his coolness.

"Then how do you know it?" she murmured.

"I did not know it until I went into the drawing-room; now I know it—now I see and know all things, and can do all things."

The sergeant was overcome with amazement.

"Very well then, save him, save him, dear!" cried the girl, flinging herself at Castanier's feet. "If nothing is impossible to you, save him! I will love you, I will adore you, I will be your slave and not your mistress. I will obey your wildest whims; you shall do as you will with me. Yes, yes, I will give you more than love; you shall have a daughter's devotion as well as . . . Rodolphe! why will you not understand! After all, however violent my passions may be, I shall be yours for ever! What should I say to persuade you? I will invent pleasures . . . I . . . Great heavens! one moment! whatever you shall ask of me—to fling myself from the window for instance—you will need to say but one word, 'Leon!' and I will plunge down into hell. I would bear any torture, any pain of body or soul, anything you might inflict upon me!"

Castanier heard her with indifference. For an answer, he indicated Leon to her with a fiendish laugh.

"The guillotine is waiting for him," he repeated.

"No, no, no! He shall not leave this house. I will save him!" she cried. "Yes; I will kill any one who lays a finger upon him! Why will you not save him?" she shrieked aloud; her eyes were blazing, her hair unbound. "Can you save him?"

"I can do everything."

"Why do you not save him?"

"Why?" shouted Castanier, and his voice made the ceiling ring.—"Eh! it is my revenge! Doing evil is my trade!"

"Die?" said Aquilina; "must he die, my lover? Is it possible?"

She sprang up and snatched a stiletto from a basket that stood on the chest of drawers and went to Castanier, who now began to laugh.

"You know very well that steel cannot hurt me now—"

Aquilina's arm suddenly dropped like a snapped harp string.

"Out with you, my good friend," said the cashier, turning to the sergeant, "and go about your business."

He held out his hand; the other felt Castanier's superior power, and could not choose but to obey.

"This house is mine; I could send for the commissary of police if I chose, and give you up as a man who has hidden himself on my premises, but I would rather let you go; I am a fiend, I am not a spy."

"I shall follow him!" said Aquilina.

"Then follow him," returned Castanier.—"Here, Jenny—"

Jenny appeared.

"Tell the porter to hail a cab for them.—Here Naqui," said Castanier, drawing a bundle of bank-notes from his pocket; "you shall not go away like a pauper from a man who loves you still."

He held out three hundred thousand francs. Aquilina took the notes, flung them on the floor, spat on them, and trampled upon them in a frenzy of despair.

"We will leave this house on foot," she cried, "without a farthing of your money.—Jenny, stay where you are."

"Good-evening!" answered the cashier, as he gathered up the notes again. "I have come back from my journey.—Jenny," he added, looking at the bewildered waiting-maid, "you seem to me to be a good sort of girl. You have no mistress now. Come here. This evening you shall have a master."

Aquilina, who felt safe nowhere, went at once with the sergeant to the house of one of her friends. But all Leon's movements were suspiciously watched by the police, and after a time he and three of his friends were arrested. The whole story may be found in the newspapers of that day.

Castanier felt that he had undergone a mental as well as a physical transformation. The Castanier of old no longer existed—the boy, the young Lothario, the soldier who had proved his courage, who had been tricked into a marriage and disillusioned, the cashier, the passionate lover who had committed a crime for Aquilina's sake. His inmost nature had suddenly asserted itself. His brain had expanded, his senses had developed. His thoughts comprehended the whole world; he saw all the things of earth as if he had been raised to some high pinnacle above the world.

Until that evening at the play he had loved Aquilina to distraction. Rather than give her up he would have shut his eyes to her infidelities; and now all that blind passion had passed away as a cloud vanishes in the sunlight.

Jenny was delighted to succeed to her mistress' position and fortune, and did the cashier's will in all things; but Castanier, who could read the inmost thoughts of the soul, discovered the real motive underlying this purely physical devotion. He amused himself with her, however, like a mischievous child who greedily sucks the juice of the cherry and flings away the stone. The next morning at breakfast time, when she was fully convinced that she was a lady and the mistress of the house, Castanier uttered one by one the thoughts that filled her mind as she drank her coffee.

"Do you know what you are thinking, child?" he said, smiling. "I will tell you: 'So all that lovely rosewood furniture that I coveted so much, and the pretty dresses that I used to try on, are mine now! All on easy terms that Madame refused, I do no know why. My word! if I might drive about in a carriage, have jewels and pretty things, a box at the theatre, and put something by! with me he should lead a life of pleasure fit to kill him if he were not as strong as a Turk! I never saw such a man!'—Was not that just what you were thinking," he went on, and something in his voice made Jenny turn pale. "Well, yes, child; you could not stand it, and I am sending you away for your own good; you would perish in the attempt. Come, let us part good friends," and he coolly dismissed her with a very small sum of money.

The first use that Castanier had promised himself that he would make of the terrible power brought at the price of his eternal happiness, was the full and complete indulgence of all his tastes.

He first put his affairs in order, readily settled his accounts with M. de Nucingen, who found a worthy German to succeed him, and then determined on a carouse worthy of the palmiest days of the Roman Empire. He plunged into dissipation as recklessly as Belshazzar of old went to that last feast in Babylon. Like Belshazzar, he saw clearly through his revels a gleaming hand that traced his doom in letters of flame, not on the narrow walls of the banqueting-chamber, but over the vast spaces of heaven that the rainbow spans. His feast was not, indeed, an orgy confined within the limits of a banquet, for he squandered all the powers of soul and body in exhausting all the pleasures of earth. The table was in some sort earth itself, the earth that trembled beneath his feet. His was the last festival of the reckless spendthrift who has thrown all prudence to the winds. The devil had given him the key of the storehouse of human pleasures; he had filled and refilled his hands, and he was fast nearing the bottom. In a moment he had felt all that that enormous power could accomplish; in a moment he had exercised it, proved it, wearied of it. What had hitherto been the sum of human desires became as nothing. So often it happens that with possession the vast poetry of desire must end, and the thing possessed is seldom the thing that we dreamed of.

Beneath Melmoth's omnipotence lurked this tragical anticlimax of so many a passion, and now the inanity of human nature was revealed to his successor, to whom infinite power brought Nothingness as a dowry.

To come to a clear understanding of Castanier's strange position, it must be borne in mind how suddenly these revolutions of thought and feeling had been wrought; how quickly they had succeeded each other; and of these things it is hard to give any idea to those who have never broken the prison bonds of time, and space, and distance. His relation to the world without had been entirely changed with the expansion of his faculties.

Like Melmoth himself, Castanier could travel in a few moments over the fertile plains of India, could soar on the wings of demons above African desert spaces, or skim the surface of the seas. The same insight that could read the inmost thoughts of others, could apprehend at a glance the nature of any material object, just as he caught as it were all flavors at once upon his tongue. He took his pleasure like a despot; a blow of the axe felled the tree that he might eat its fruits. The transitions, the alternations that measure joy and pain, and diversify human happiness, no longer existed for him. He had so completely glutted his appetites that pleasure must overpass the limits of pleasure to tickle a palate cloyed with satiety, and suddenly grown fastidious beyond all measure, so that ordinary pleasures became distasteful. Conscious that at will he was the master of all the women that he could desire, knowing that his power was irresistible, he did not care to exercise it; they were pliant to his unexpressed wishes, to his most extravagant caprices, until he felt a horrible thirst for love, and would have love beyond their power to give.

The world refused him nothing save faith and prayer, the soothing and consoling love that is not of this world. He was obeyed—it was a horrible position.

The torrents of pain, and pleasure, and thought that shook his soul and his bodily frame would have overwhelmed the strongest human being; but in him there was a power of vitality proportioned to the power of the sensations that assailed him. He felt within him a vague immensity of longing that earth could not satisfy. He spent his days on outspread wings, longing to traverse the luminous fields of space to other spheres that he knew afar by intuitive perception, a clear and hopeless knowledge. His soul dried up within him, for he hungered and thirsted after things that can neither be drunk nor eaten, but for which he could not choose but crave. His lips, like Melmoth's, burned with desire; he panted for the unknown, for he knew all things.

The mechanism and the scheme of the world was apparent to him, and its working interested him no longer; he did not long disguise the profound scorn that makes of a man of extraordinary powers a sphinx who knows everything and says nothing, and sees all things with an unmoved countenance. He felt not the slightest wish to communicate his knowledge to other men. He was rich with all the wealth of the world, with one effort he could make the circle of the globe, and riches and power were meaningless for him. He felt the awful melancholy of omnipotence, a melancholy which Satan and God relieve by the exercise of infinite power in mysterious ways known to them alone. Castanier had not, like his Master, the inextinguishable energy of hate and malice; he felt that he was a devil, but a devil whose time was not yet come, while Satan is a devil through all eternity, and being damned beyond redemption, delights to stir up the world, like a dung heap, with his triple fork and to thwart therein the designs of God. But Castanier, for his misfortune, had one hope left.

If in a moment he could move from one pole to the other as a bird springs restlessly from side to side in its cage, when, like the bird, he has crossed his prison, he saw the vast immensity of space beyond it. That vision of the Infinite left him for ever unable to see humanity and its affairs as other men saw them. The insensate fools who long for the power of the Devil gauge its desirability from a human standpoint; they do not see that with the Devil's power they will likewise assume his thoughts, and that they will be doomed to remain as men among creatures who will no longer understand them. The Nero unknown to history who dreams of setting Paris on fire for his private entertainment, like an exhibition of a burning house on the boards of a theatre, does not suspect that if he had the power, Paris would become for him as little interesting as an ant-heap by the roadside to a hurrying passer-by. The circle of the sciences was for Castanier something like a logogriph for a man who does not know the key to it. Kings and Governments were despicable in his eyes. His great debauch had been in some sort a deplorable farewell to his life as a man. The earth had grown too narrow for him, for the infernal gifts laid bare for him the secrets of creation—he saw the cause and foresaw its end. He was shut out from all that men call "heaven" in all languages under the sun; he could no longer think of heaven.

Then he came to understand the look on his predecessor's face and the drying up of the life within; then he knew all that was meant by the baffled hope that gleamed in Melmoth's eyes; he, too, knew the thirst that burned those red lips, and the agony of a continual struggle between two natures grown to giant size. Even yet he might be an angel, and he knew himself to be a fiend. His was the fate of a sweet and gentle creature that a wizard's malice has imprisoned in a mis-shapen form, entrapping it by a pact, so that another's will must set it free from its detested envelope.

As a deception only increases the ardor with which a man of really great nature explores the infinite of sentiment in a woman's heart, so Castanier awoke to find that one idea lay like a weight upon his soul, an idea which was perhaps the key to loftier spheres. The very fact that he had bartered away his eternal happiness led him to dwell in thought upon the future of those who pray and believe. On the morrow of his debauch, when he entered into the sober possession of his power, this idea made him feel himself a prisoner; he knew the burden of the woe that poets, and prophets, and great oracles of faith have set forth for us in such mighty words; he felt the point of the Flaming Sword plunged into his side, and hurried in search of Melmoth. What had become of his predecessor?

The Englishman was living in a mansion in the Rue Ferou, near Saint-Sulpice—a gloomy, dark, damp, and cold abode. The Rue Ferou itself is one of the most dismal streets in Paris; it has a north aspect like all the streets that lie at right angles to the left bank of the Seine, and the houses are in keeping with the site. As Castanier stood on the threshold he found that the door itself, like the vaulted roof, was hung with black; rows of lighted tapers shone brilliantly as though some king were lying in state; and a priest stood on either side of a catafalque that had been raised there.

"There is no need to ask why you have come, sir," the old hall porter said to Castanier; "you are so like our poor dear master that is gone. But if you are his brother, you have come too late to bid him good-bye. The good gentleman died the night before last."

"How did he die?" Castanier asked of one of the priests.

"Set your mind at rest," said the old priest; he partly raised as he spoke the black pall that covered the catafalque.

Castanier, looking at him, saw one of those faces that faith has made sublime; the soul seemed to shine forth from every line of it, bringing light and warmth for other men, kindled by the unfailing charity within. This was Sir John Melmoth's confessor.

"Your brother made an end that men may envy, and that must rejoice the angels. Do you know what joy there is in heaven over a sinner that repents? His tears of penitence, excited by grace, flowed without ceasing; death alone checked them. The Holy Spirit dwelt in him. His burning words, full of lively faith, were worthy of the Prophet-King. If, in the course of my life, I have never heard a more dreadful confession than from the lips of this Irish gentleman, I have likewise never heard such fervent and passionate prayers. However great the measures of his sins may have been, his repentance has filled the abyss to overflowing. The hand of God was visibly stretched out above him, for he was completely changed, there was such heavenly beauty in his face. The hard eyes were softened by tears; the resonant voice that struck terror into those who heard it took the tender and compassionate tones of those who themselves have passed through deep humiliation. He so edified those who heard his words, that some who had felt drawn to see the spectacle of a Christian's death fell on their knees as he spoke of heavenly things, and of the infinite glory of God, and gave thanks and praise to Him. If he is leaving no worldly wealth to his family, no family can possess a greater blessing than this that he surely gained for them, a soul among the blessed, who will watch over you all and direct you in the path to heaven."

These words made such a vivid impression upon Castanier that he instantly hurried from the house to the Church of Saint-Sulpice, obeying what might be called a decree of fate. Melmoth's repentance had stupefied him.

At that time, on certain mornings in the week, a preacher, famed for his eloquence, was wont to hold conferences, in the course of which he demonstrated the truths of the Catholic faith for the youth of a generation proclaimed to be indifferent in matters of belief by another voice no less eloquent than his own.

The conference had been put off to a later hour on account of Melmoth's funeral, so Castanier arrived just as the great preacher was epitomizing the proofs of a future existence of happiness with all the charm of eloquence and force of expression which have made him famous. The seeds of divine doctrine fell into a soil prepared for them in the old dragoon, into whom the Devil had glided. Indeed, if there is a phenomenon well attested by experience, is it not the spiritual phenomenon commonly called "the faith of the peasant"? The strength of belief varies inversely with the amount of use that a man has made of his reasoning faculties. Simple people and soldiers belong to the unreasoning class. Those who have marched through life beneath the banner of instinct are far more ready to receive the light than minds and hearts overwearied with the world's sophistries.

Castanier had the southern temperament; he had joined the army as a lad of sixteen, and had followed the French flag till he was nearly forty years old. As a common trooper, he had fought day and night, and day after day, and, as in duty bound, had thought of his horse first, and of himself afterwards. While he served his military apprenticeship, therefore, he had but little leisure in which to reflect on the destiny of man, and when he became an officer he had his men to think of. He had been swept from battlefield to battlefield, but he had never thought of what comes after death. A soldier's life does not demand much thinking. Those who cannot understand the lofty political ends involved and the interests of nation and nation; who cannot grasp political schemes as well as plans of campaign, and combine the science of the tactician with that of the administrator, are bound to live in a state of ignorance; the most boorish peasant in the most backward district in France is scarcely in a worse case. Such men as these bear the brunt of war, yield passive obedience to the brain that directs them, and strike down the men opposed to them as the woodcutter fells timber in the forest. Violent physical exertion is succeeded by times of inertia, when they repair the waste. They fight and drink, fight and eat, fight and sleep, that they may the better deal hard blows; the powers of the mind are not greatly exercised in this turbulent round of existence, and the character is as simple as heretofore.

When the men who have shown such energy on the battlefield return to ordinary civilization, most of those who have not risen to high rank seem to have acquired no ideas, and to have no aptitude, no capacity, for grasping new ideas.

To the utter amazement of a younger generation, those who made our armies so glorious and so terrible are as simple as children, and as slow-witted as a clerk at his worst, and the captain of a thundering squadron is scarcely fit to keep a merchant's day-book. Old soldiers of this stamp, therefore being innocent of any attempt to use their reasoning faculties, act upon their strongest impulses. Castanier's crime was one of those matters that raise so many questions, that, in order to debate about it, a moralist might call for its "discussion by clauses," to make use of a parliamentary expression.

Passion had counseled the crime; the cruelly irresistible power of feminine witchery had driven him to commit it; no man can say of himself, "I will never do that," when a siren joins in the combat and throws her spells over him.

So the word of life fell upon a conscience newly awakened to the truths of religion which the French Revolution and a soldier's career had forced Castanier to neglect. The solemn words, "You will be happy or miserable for all eternity!" made but the more terrible impression upon him, because he had exhausted earth and shaken it like a barren tree; because his desires could effect all things, so that it was enough that any spot in earth or heaven should be forbidden him, and he forthwith thought of nothing else. If it were allowable to compare such great things with social follies, Castanier's position was not unlike that of a banker who, finding that his all-powerful millions cannot obtain for him an entrance into the society of the noblesse, must set his heart upon entering that circle, and all the social privileges that he has already acquired are as nothing in his eyes from the moment when he discovers that a single one is lacking.

Here is a man more powerful than all the kings on earth put together; a man who, like Satan, could wrestle with God Himself; leaning against one of the pillars in the Church of Saint-Sulpice, weighed down by the feelings and thoughts that oppressed him, and absorbed in the thought of a Future, the same thought that had engulfed Melmoth.

"He was very happy, was Melmoth!" cried Castanier. "He died in the certain knowledge that he would go to heaven."

In a moment the greatest possible change had been wrought in the cashier's ideas. For several days he had been a devil, now he was nothing but a man; an image of the fallen Adam, of the sacred tradition embodied in all cosmogonies. But while he had thus shrunk he retained a germ of greatness, he had been steeped in the Infinite. The power of hell had revealed the divine power. He thirsted for heaven as he had never thirsted after the pleasures of earth, that are so soon exhausted. The enjoyments which the fiend promises are but the enjoyments of earth on a larger scale, but to the joys of heaven there is no limit. He believed in God, and the spell that gave him the treasures of the world was as nothing to him now; the treasures themselves seemed to him as contemptible as pebbles to an admirer of diamonds; they were but gewgaws compared with the eternal glories of the other life. A curse lay, he thought, on all things that came to him from this source. He sounded dark depths of painful thought as he listened to the service performed for Melmoth. The *Dies irae* filled him with awe; he felt all the grandeur of that cry of a repentant soul trembling before the Throne of God. The Holy Spirit, like a devouring flame, passed through him as fire consumes straw.

The tears were falling from his eyes when—"Are you a relation of the dead?" the beadle asked him.

"I am his heir," Castanier answered.

"Give something for the expenses of the services!" cried the man.

"No," said the cashier. (The Devil's money should not go to the Church.)

"For the poor!"

"No."

"For repairing the Church!"

"No."

"The Lady Chapel!"

"No."

"For the schools!"

"No."

Castanier went, not caring to expose himself to the sour looks that the irritated functionaries gave him.

Outside, in the street, he looked up at the Church of Saint-Sulpice. "What made people build the giant cathedrals I have seen in every country?" he asked himself. "The feeling shared so widely throughout all time must surely be based upon something."

"Something! Do you call God *something?*" cried his conscience. "God! God! God! . . ."

The word was echoed and re-echoed by an inner voice, til it overwhelmed him; but his feeling of terror subsided as he heard sweet distant sounds of music that he had caught faintly before. They were singing in the church, he thought, and his eyes scanned the great doorway. But as he listened more closely, the sounds poured upon him from all sides; he looked round the square, but there was no sign of any musicians. The melody brought visions of a distant heaven and far-off gleams of hope; but it also quickened the remorse that had set the lost soul in a ferment. He went on his way through Paris, walking as men walk who are crushed beneath the burden of their sorrow, seeing everything with unseeing eyes, loitering like an idler, stopping without cause, muttering to himself, careless of the traffic, making no effort to avoid a blow from a plank of timber.

Imperceptibly repentance brought him under the influence of the divine grace that soothes while it bruises the heart so terribly. His face came to wear a look of Melmoth, something great, with a trace of madness in the greatness—a look of dull and hopeless distress, mingled with the excited eagerness of hope, and, beneath it all, a gnawing sense of loathing for all that the world can give. The humblest of prayers lurked in the eyes that saw with such dreadful clearness. His power was the measure of his anguish. His body was bowed down by the fearful storm that shook his soul, as the tall pines bend before the blast. Like his predecessor, he could not refuse to bear the burden of life; he was afraid to die while he bore the yoke of hell. The torment grew intolerable.

At last, one morning, he bethought himself how that Melmoth (now among the blessed) had made the proposal of an exchange, and how that he had accepted it; others, doubtless, would follow his example; for in an age proclaimed, by the inheritors of the eloquence of the Fathers of the Church, to be fatally indifferent to religion, it should be easy to find a man who would accept the conditions of the contract in order to prove its advantages.

"There is one place where you can learn what kings will fetch in the market; where nations are weighed in the balance and systems appraised; where the value of a government is stated in terms of the five-franc piece; where ideas and beliefs have their price, and everything is discounted; where God Himself, in a manner, borrows on the security of His revenue of souls, for the Pope has a running account there. Is it not there that I should go to traffic in souls?"

Castanier went quite joyously on 'Change, thinking that it would be as easy to buy a soul as to invest money in the Funds. Any ordinary person would have feared ridicule, but Castanier knew by experience that a desperate man takes everything seriously. A prisoner lying under sentence of death would listen to the madman who should tell him that by pronouncing some gibberish he could escape through the keyhole; for suffering is credulous, and clings to an idea until it fails, as the swimmer borne along by the current clings to the branch that snaps in his hand.

Towards four o'clock that afternoon Castanier appeared among the little knots of men who were transacting private business after 'Change. He was personally known to some of the brokers; and while affecting to be in search of an acquaintance, he managed to pick up the current gossip and rumors of failure.

"Catch me negotiating bills for Claparon & Co., my boy. The bank collector went round to return their acceptances to them this morning," said a fat banker in his outspoken way. "If you have any of their paper, look out."

Claparon was in the building, in deep consultation with a man well known for the ruinous rate at which he lent money. Castanier went forthwith in search of the said Claparon, a merchant who had a reputation for taking heavy risks that meant wealth or utter ruin. The money-lender walked away as Castanier came up. A gesture betrayed the speculator's despair.

"Well, Claparon, the Bank wants a hundred thousand francs of you, and it is four o'clock; the thing is known, and it is too late to arrange your little failure comfortably," said Castanier.

"Sir!"

"Speak lower," the cashier went on. "How if I were to propose a piece of business that would bring you in as much money as you require?"

"It would not discharge my liabilities; every business that I ever heard of wants a little time to simmer in."

"I know of something that will set you straight in a moment," answered Castanier; "but first you would have to—"

"Do what?"

"Sell your share of paradise. It is a matter of business like anything else, isn't it? We all hold shares in the great Speculation of Eternity."

"I tell you this," said Claparon angrily, "that I am just the man to lend you a slap in the face. When a man is in trouble, it is no time to pay silly jokes on him."

"I am talking seriously," said Castanier, and he drew a bundle of notes from his pocket.

"In the first place," said Claparon, "I am not going to sell my soul to the Devil for a trifle. I want five hundred thousand francs before I strike—"

"Who talks of stinting you?" asked Castanier, cutting him short. "You shall have more gold than you could stow in the cellars of the Bank of France."

He held out a handful of notes. That decided Claparon.

"Done," he cried; "but how is the bargain to be make?"

"Let us go over yonder, no one is standing there," said Castanier, pointing to a corner of the court.

Claparon and his tempter exchanged a few words, with their faces turned to the wall. None of the onlookers guessed the nature of this by-play, though their curiosity was keenly excited by the strange gestures of the two contracting parties. When Castanier returned, there was a sudden outburst of amazed exclamation. As in the Assembly where the least event immediately attracts attention, all faces were turned to the two men who had caused the sensation, and a shiver passed through all beholders at the change that had taken place in them.

The men who form the moving crowd that fills the Stock Exchange are soon known to each other by sight. They watch each other like players round a card-table. Some shrewd observers can tell how a man will play and the condition of his exchequer from a survey of his face; and the Stock Exchange is simply a vast card-table. Every one, therefore, had noticed Claparon and Castanier. The latter (like the Irishman before him) had been muscular and powerful, his eyes were full of light, his color high. The dignity and power in his face had struck awe into them all; they wondered how old Castanier had come by it; and now they beheld Castanier divested of his power, shrunken, wrinkled, aged, and feeble. He had drawn Claparon out of the crowd with the energy of a sick man in a fever fit; he had looked like an opium-eater during the brief period of excitement that the drug can give; now, on his return, he seemed to be in the condition of utter exhaustion in which the patient dies after the fever departs, or to be suffering from the horrible prostration that follows on excessive indulgence in the delights of narcotics. The infernal power that had upheld him through his debauches had left him, and the body was left unaided and alone to endure the agony of remorse and the heavy burden of sincere repentance. Claparon's troubles every one could guess; but Claparon reappeared, on the other hand, with sparkling eyes, holding his head high with the pride of Lucifer. The crisis had passed from the one man to the other.

"Now you can drop off with an easy mind, old man," said Claparon to Castanier.

"For pity's sake, send for a cab and for a priest; send for the curate of Saint-Sulpice!" answered the old dragoon, sinking down upon the curbstone.

The words "a priest" reached the ears of several people, and produced uproarious jeering among the stockbrokers, for faith with these gentlemen means a belief that a scrap of paper called a mortgage represents an estate, and the List of Fundholders is their Bible.

"Shall I have time to repent?" said Castanier to himself, in a piteous voice, that impressed Claparon.

A cab carried away the dying man; the speculator went to the bank at once to meet his bills; and the momentary sensation produced upon the throng of business men by the sudden change on the two faces, vanished like the furrow cut by a ship's keel in the sea. News of the greatest importance kept the attention of the world of commerce on the alert; and when commercial interests are at stake, Moses might appear with his two luminous horns, and his coming would scarcely receive the honors of a pun, the gentlemen whose business it is to write the Market Reports would ignore his existence.

When Claparon had made his payments, fear seized upon him. There was no mistake about his power. He went on 'Change again, and offered his bargain to other men in embarrassed circumstances. The Devil's bond, "together with the rights, easements, and privileges appertaining thereunto,"—to use the expression of the notary who succeeded Claparon, changed hands for the sum of seven hundred thousand francs. The notary in his turn parted with the agreement with the Devil for five hundred thousand francs to a building contractor in difficulties, who likewise was rid of it to an iron merchant in consideration of a hundred thousand crowns. In fact, by five o'clock people had ceased to believe in the strange contract, and purchasers were lacking for want of confidence.

At half-past five the holder of the bond was a house-painter, who was lounging by the door of the building in the Rue Feydeau, where at that time stockbrokers temporarily congregated. The house-painter, simple fellow, could not think what was the matter with him. He "felt all anyhow"; so he told his wife when he went home.

The Rue Feydeau, as idlers about town are aware, is a place of pilgrimage for youths who for lack of a mistress bestow their ardent affection upon the whole sex. On the first floor of the most rigidly respectable domicile therein dwelt one of those exquisite creatures whom it has pleased heaven to endow with the rarest and most surpassing beauty. As it is impossible that they should all be duchesses or queens (since there are many more pretty women in the world than titles and thrones for them to adorn), they are content to make a stockbroker or a banker happy at a fixed price. To this good-natured beauty, Euphrasia by name, an unbounded ambition had led a notary's clerk to aspire. In short, the second clerk in the office of Maitre Crottat, notary, had fallen in love with her, as youth at two-and-twenty can fall in love. The scrivener would have murdered the Pope and run amuck through the whole sacred college to procure the miserable sum of a hundred louis to pay for a shawl which had turned Euphrasia's head, at which price her waiting-woman had promised that Euphrasia should be his. The infatuated youth walked to and fro under Madame Euphrasia's windows, like the polar bears in their cage at the Jardin des Plantes, with his right hand thrust beneath his waistcoat in the region of the heart, which he was fit to tear from his bosom, but as yet he had only wrenched at the elastic of his braces.

"What can one do to raise ten thousand francs?" he asked himself. "Shall I make off with the money that I must pay on the registration of that conveyance? Good heavens! my loan would not ruin the purchaser, a man with seven millions! And then next day I would fling myself at his feet and say, 'I have taken ten thousand francs belonging to you, sir; I am twenty-two years of age, and I am in love with Euphrasia—that is my story. My father is rich, he will pay you back; do not ruin me! Have not you yourself been twenty-two years old and madly in love?' But these beggarly landowners have no souls! He would be quite likely to give me up to the public prosecutor, instead of taking pity upon me. Good God! if it were only possible to sell your soul to the Devil! But there is neither a God nor a Devil; it is all nonsense out of nursery tales and old wives' talk. What shall I do?"

"If you have a mind to sell your soul to the Devil, sir," said the house-painter, who had overheard something that the clerk let fall, "you can have the ten thousand francs."

"And Euphrasia!" cried the clerk, as he struck a bargain with the devil that inhabited the house-painter.

The pact concluded, the frantic clerk went to find the shawl, and mounted Madame Euphrasia's staircase; and as (literally) the devil was in him, he did not come down for twelve days, drowning the thought of hell and of his privileges in twelve days of love and riot and forgetfulness, for which he had bartered away all his hopes of a paradise to come.

And in this way the secret of the vast power discovered and acquired by the Irishman, the offspring of Maturin's brain, was lost to mankind; and the various Orientalists, Mystics, and Archaeologists who take an interest in these matters were unable to hand down to posterity the proper method of invoking the Devil, for the following sufficient reasons:

On the thirteenth day after these frenzied nuptials the wretched clerk lay on a pallet bed in a garret in his master's house in the Rue Saint-Honore. Shame, the stupid goddess who dares not behold herself, had taken possession of the young man. He had fallen ill; he would nurse himself; misjudged the quantity of a remedy devised by the skill of a practitioner well known on the walls of Paris, and succumbed to the effects of an overdose of mercury. His corpse was as black as a mole's back. A devil had left unmistakable traces of its passage there; could it have been Ashtaroth?

"The estimable youth to whom you refer has been carried away to the planet Mercury," said the head clerk to a German demonologist who came to investigate the matter at first hand.

"I am quite prepared to believe it," answered the Teuton.

"Oh!"

"Yes, sir," returned the other. "The opinion you advance coincides with the very words of Jacob Boehme. In the forty-eighth proposition of *The Threefold Life of Man* he says that 'if God hath brought all things to pass with a LET THERE BE, the FIAT is the secret matrix which comprehends and apprehends the nature which is formed by the spirit born of Mercury and of God.'"

"What do you say, sir?"

The German delivered his quotation afresh.

"We do not know it," said the clerks.

"*Fiat?* . . ." said a clerk. "*Fiat lux!*"

"You can verify the citation for yourselves," said the German. "You will find the passage in the *Treatise of the Threefold Life of Man*, page 75; the edition was published by M. Migneret in 1809. It was translated into French by a philosopher who had a great admiration for the famous shoemaker."

"Oh! he was a shoemaker, was he?" said the head clerk.

"In Prussia," said the German.

"Did he work for the King of Prussia?" inquired a Boeotian of a second clerk.

"He must have vamped up his prose," said a third.

"That man is colossal!" cried the fourth, pointing to the Teuton.

That gentleman, though a demonologist of the first rank, did not know the amount of devilry to be found in a notary's clerk. He went away without the least idea that they were making game of him, and fully under the impression that the young fellows regarded Boehme as a colossal genius.

"Education is making strides in France," said he to himself.

PARIS, May 6, 1835.

ADDENDUM

The following personages appear in other stories of the Human Comedy.

Aquilina
   The Magic Skin

Claparon, Charles
   A Bachelor's Establishment
   Cesar Birotteau
   The Firm of Nucingen
   A Man of Business
   The Middle Classes

Euphrasia
   The Magic Skin

Nucingen, Baronne Delphine de
   Father Goriot
   The Thirteen
   Eugenie Grandet
   Cesar Birotteau
   Lost Illusions
   A Distinguished Provincial at Paris
   The Commission in Lunacy
   Scenes from a Courtesan's Life
   Modeste Mignon
   The Firm of Nucingen
   Another Study of Woman
   A Daughter of Eve

The Member for Arcis

Tillet, Ferdinand du
　Cesar Birotteau
　The Firm of Nucingen
　The Middle Classes
　A Bachelor's Establishment
　Pierrette
　A Distinguished Provencial at Paris
　The Secrets of a Princess
　A Daughter of Eve
　The Member for Arcis
　Cousin Betty
　The Unconscious Humorists

UNCONSCIOUS COMEDIANS

Translated by
Katharine Prescott Wormeley

DEDICATION

To Monsieur le Comte Jules de Castellane.

Leon de Lora, our celebrated landscape painter, belongs to one of the noblest families of the Roussillon (Spanish originally) which, although distinguished for the antiquity of its race, has been doomed for a century to the proverbial poverty of hidalgos. Coming, light-footed, to Paris from the department of the Eastern Pyrenees, with the sum of eleven francs in his pocket for all viaticum, he had in some degree forgotten the miseries and privations of his childhood and his family amid the other privations and miseries which are never lacking to "rapins," whose whole fortune consists of intrepid vocation. Later, the cares of fame and those of success were other causes of forgetfulness.

If you have followed the capricious and meandering course of these studies, perhaps you will remember Mistigris, Schinner's pupil, one of the heroes of "A Start in Life" (Scenes from Private Life), and his brief apparitions in other Scenes. In 1845, this landscape painter, emulator of the Hobbemas, Ruysdaels, and Lorraines, resembles no more the shabby, frisky rapin whom we then knew. Now an illustrious man, he owns a charming house in the rue de Berlin, not far from the hotel de Brambourg, where his friend Brideau lives, and quite close to the house of Schinner, his early master. He is a member of the Institute and an officer of the Legion of honor; he is thirty-six years old, has an income of twenty thousand francs from the Funds, his pictures sell for their weight in gold, and (what seems to him more extraordinary than the invitations he receives occasionally to court balls) his name and fame, mentioned so often for the last sixteen years by the press of Europe, has at last penetrated to the valley of the Eastern Pyrenees, where vegetate three veritable Loras: his father, his eldest brother, and an old paternal aunt, Mademoiselle Urraca y Lora.

In the maternal line the painter has no relation left except a cousin, the nephew of his mother, residing in a small manufacturing town in the department. This cousin was the first to bethink himself of Leon. But it was not until 1840 that Leon de Lora received a letter from Monsieur Sylvestre Palafox-Castal-Gazonal (called simply Gazonal) to which he replied that he was assuredly himself,—that is to say, the son of the late Leonie Gazonal, wife of Comte Fernand Didas y Lora.

During the summer of 1841 cousin Sylvestre Gazonal went to inform the illustrious unknown family of Lora that their little Leon had not gone to the Rio de la Plata, as they supposed, but was now one of the greatest geniuses of the French school of painting; a fact the family did not believe. The eldest son, Don Juan de Lora assured his cousin Gazonal that he was certainly the dupe of some Parisian wag.

Now the said Gazonal was intending to go to Paris to prosecute a lawsuit which the prefect of the Eastern Pyrenees had arbitrarily removed from the usual jurisdiction, transferring it to that of the Council of State. The worthy provincial determined to investigate this act, and to ask his Parisian cousin the reason of such high-handed measures. It thus happened that Monsieur Gazonal came to Paris, took shabby lodgings in the rue Croix-des-Petits-Champs, and was amazed to see the palace of his cousin in the rue de Berlin. Being told that the painter was then travelling in Italy, he renounced, for the time being, the intention of asking his advice, and doubted if he should ever find his maternal relationship acknowledged by so great a man.

During the years 1843 and 1844 Gazonal attended to his lawsuit. This suit concerned a question as to the current and level of a stream of water and the necessity of removing a dam, in which dispute the administration, instigated by the abutters on the river banks, had meddled. The removal of the dam threatened the existence of Gazonal's manufactory. In 1845, Gazonal considered his cause as wholly lost; the secretary of the Master of Petitions, charged with the duty of drawing up the report, had confided to him that the said report would assuredly be against him, and his own lawyer confirmed the statement. Gazonal, though commander of the National Guard in his own town and one of the most capable manufacturers of the department, found himself of so little account in Paris, and he was, moreover, so frightened by the costs of living and the dearness of even the most trifling things, that he kept himself, all this time, secluded in his shabby lodgings. The Southerner, deprived of his sun, execrated Paris, which he called a manufactory of rheumatism. As he added up the costs of his suit and his living, he vowed within himself to poison the prefect on his return, or to minotaurize him. In his moments of deepest sadness he killed the prefect outright; in gayer mood he contented himself with minotaurizing him.

One morning as he ate his breakfast and cursed his fate, he picked up a newspaper savagely. The following lines, ending an article, struck Gazonal as if the mysterious voice which speaks to gamblers before they win had sounded in his ear: "Our celebrated landscape painter, Leon de Lora, lately returned from Italy, will exhibit several pictures at the Salon; thus the exhibition promises, as we see, to be most brilliant." With the suddenness of action that distinguishes the sons of the sunny South, Gazonal sprang from his lodgings to the street, from the street to a street-cab, and drove to the rue de Berlin to find his cousin.

Leon de Lora sent word by a servant to his cousin Gazonal that he invited him to breakfast the next day at the Cafe de Paris, but he was now engaged in a matter which did not allow him to receive his cousin at the present moment. Gazonal, like a true Southerner, recounted all his troubles to the valet.

The next day at ten o'clock, Gazonal, much too well-dressed for the occasion (he had put on his bottle-blue coat with brass buttons, a frilled shirt, a white waistcoat and yellow gloves), awaited his amphitryon a full hour, stamping his feet on the boulevard, after hearing from the master of the cafe that "these gentlemen" breakfasted habitually between eleven and twelve o'clock.

"Between eleven and half-past," he said when he related his adventures to his cronies in the provinces, "two Parisians dressed in simple frock-coats, looking like *nothing at all*, called out when they saw me on the boulevard, 'There's our Gazonal!'"

The speaker was Bixiou, with whom Leon de Lora had armed himself to "bring out" his provincial cousin, in other words, to make him pose.

"'Don't be vexed, cousin, I'm at your service!' cried out that little Leon, taking me in his arms," related Gazonal on his return home. "The breakfast was splendid. I thought I was going blind when I saw the number of bits of gold it took to pay that bill. Those fellows must earn their weight in gold, for I saw my cousin give the waiter *thirty sous*—the price of a whole day's work!"

During this monstrous breakfast—advisedly so called in view of six dozen Osten oysters, six cutlets a la Soubise, a chicken a la Marengo, lobster mayonnaise, green peas, a mushroom pasty, washed down with three bottles of Bordeaux, three bottles of Champagne, plus coffee and liqueurs, to say nothing of relishes—Gazonal was magnificent in his diatribes against Paris. The worthy manufacturer complained of the length of the four-pound bread-loaves, the height of the houses, the indifference of the passengers in the streets to one another, the cold, the rain, the cost of hackney-coaches, all of which and much else he bemoaned in so witty a manner that the two artists took a mighty fancy to cousin Gazonal, and made him relate his lawsuit from beginning to end.

"My lawsuit," he said in his Southern accent and rolling his r's, "is a very simple thing; they want my manufactory. I've employed here in Paris a dolt of a lawyer, to whom I give twenty francs every time he opens an eye, and he is always asleep. He's a slug, who drives in his coach, while I go afoot and he splashes me. I see now I ought to have had a carriage! On the other hand, that Council of State are a pack of do-nothings, who leave their duties to little scamps every one of whom is bought up by our prefect. That's my lawsuit! They want my manufactory! Well, they'll get it! and they must manage the best they can with my workmen, a hundred of 'em, who'll make them sing another tune before they've done with them."

"Two years. Ha! that meddling prefect! he shall pay dear for this; I'll have his life if I have to give mine on the scaffold—"

"Which state councillor presides over your section?"

"A former newspaper man,—doesn't pay ten sous in taxes,—his name is Massol."

The two Parisians exchanged glances.

"Who is the commissioner who is making the report?"

"Ha! that's still more queer; he's Master of Petitions, professor of something or other at the Sorbonne,—a fellow who writes things in reviews, and for whom I have the profoundest contempt."

"Claude Vignon," said Bixiou.

"Yes, that's his name," replied Gazonal. "Massol and Vignon—there you have Social Reason, in which there's no reason at all."

"There must be some way out of it," said Leon de Lora. "You see, cousin, all things are possible in Paris for good as well as for evil, for the just as well as the unjust. There's nothing that can't be done, undone, and redone."

"The devil take me if I stay ten days more in this hole of a place, the dullest in all France!"

The two cousins and Bixiou were at this moment walking from one end to the other of that sheet of asphalt on which, between the hours of one and three, it is difficult to avoid seeing some of the personages in honor of whom Fame puts one or the other of her trumpets to her lips. Formerly that locality was the Place Royale; next it was the Pont Neuf; in these days this privilege had been acquired by the Boulevard des Italiens.

"Paris," said the painter to his cousin, "is an instrument on which we must know how to play; if we stand here ten minutes I'll give you your first lesson. There, look!" he said, raising his cane and pointing to a couple who were just then coming out from the Passage de l'Opera.

"Goodness! who's that?" asked Gazonal.

That was an old woman, in a bonnet which had spent six months in a showcase, a very pretentious gown and a faded tartan shawl, whose face had been buried twenty years of her life in a damp lodge, and whose swollen hand-bag betokened no better social position than that of an ex-portress. With her was a slim little girl, whose eyes, fringed with black lashes, had lost their innocence and showed great weariness; her face, of a pretty shape, was fresh and her hair abundant, her forehead charming but audacious, her bust thin,—in other words, an unripe fruit.

"That," replied Bixiou, "is a rat tied to its mother."

"A rat!—what's that?"

"That particular rat," said Leon, with a friendly nod to Mademoiselle Ninette, "may perhaps win your suit for you."

Gazonal bounded; but Bixiou had held him by the arm ever since they left the cafe, thinking perhaps that the flush on his face was rather vivid.

"That rat, who is just leaving a rehearsal at the Opera-house, is going home to eat a miserable dinner, and will return about three o'clock to dress, if she dances in the ballet this evening—as she will, to-day being Monday. This rat is already an old rat for she is thirteen years of age. Two years from now that creature may be worth sixty thousand francs; she will be all or nothing, a great danseuse or a marcheuse, a celebrated person or a vulgar courtesan. She has worked hard since she was eight years old. Such as you see her, she is worn out with fatigue; she exhausted her body this morning in the dancing-class, she is just leaving a rehearsal where the evolutions are as complicated as a Chinese puzzle; and she'll go through them again to-night. The rat is one of the primary elements of the Opera; she is to the leading danseuse what a junior clerk is to a notary. The rat is—hope."

"Who produces the rat?" asked Gazonal.

"Porters, paupers, actors, dancers," replied Bixiou. "Only the lowest depths of poverty could force a child to subject her feet and joints to positive torture, to keep herself virtuous out of mere speculation until she is eighteen years of age, and to live with some horrible old crone like a beautiful plant in a dressing of manure. You shall see now a procession defiling before you, one after the other, of men of talent, little and great, artists in seed or flower, who are raising to the glory of France that every-day monument called the Opera, an assemblage of forces, wills, and forms of genius, nowhere collected as in Paris.

"I have already seen the Opera," said Gazonal, with a self-sufficient air.

"Yes, from a three-francs-sixty-sous seat among the gods," replied the landscape painter; "just as you have seen Paris in the rue Croix-des-Petits-Champs, without knowing anything about it. What did they give at the Opera when you were there?"

"Guillaume Tell."

"Well," said Leon, "Matilde's grand DUO must have delighted you. What do you suppose that charming singer did when she left the stage?"

"She—well, what?"

"She ate two bloody mutton-chops which her servant had ready for her."

"Pooh! nonsense!"

"Malibran kept up on brandy—but it killed her in the end. Another thing! You have seen the ballet, and you'll now see it defiling past you in its every-day clothes, without knowing that the face of your lawsuit depends on a pair of those legs."

"My lawsuit!"

"See, cousin, here comes what is called a marcheuse."

Leon pointed to one of those handsome creatures who at twenty-five years of age have lived sixty, and whose beauty is so real and so sure of being cultivated that they make no display of it. She was tall, and walked well, with the arrogant look of a dandy; her toilet was remarkable for its ruinous simplicity.

"That is Carabine," said Bixiou, who gave her, as did Leon, a slight nod to which she responded by a smile.

"There's another who may possibly get your prefect turned out."

"A marcheuse!—but what is that?"

"A marcheuse is a rat of great beauty whom her mother, real or fictitious, has sold as soon as it was clear she would become neither first, second, nor third danseuse, but who prefers the occupation of coryphee to any other, for the main reason that having spent her youth in that employment she is unfitted for any other. She has been rejected at the minor theatres where they want danseuses; she has not succeeded in the three towns where ballets are given; she has not had the money, or perhaps the desire to go to foreign countries—for perhaps you don't know that the great school of dancing in Paris supplies the whole world with male and female dancers. Thus a rat who becomes a marcheuse,—that is to say, an ordinary figurante in a ballet,—must have some solid attachment which keeps her in Paris: either a rich man she does not love or a poor man she loves too well. The one you have just seen pass will probably dress and redress three times this evening,—as a princess, a peasant-girl, a Tyrolese; by which she will earn about two hundred francs a month."

"She is better dressed than my prefect's wife."

"If you should go to her house," said Bixiou, "you would find there a chamber-maid, a cook, and a man-servant. She occupies a fine apartment in the rue Saint-Georges; in short, she is, in proportion to French fortunes of the present day compared with those of former times, a relic of the eighteenth century 'opera-girl.' Carabine is a power; at this moment she governs du Tillet, a banker who is very influential in the Chamber of Deputies."

"And above these two rounds in the ballet ladder what comes next?" asked Gazonal.

"Look!" said his cousin, pointing to an elegant caleche which was turning at that moment from the boulevard into the rue Grange-Bateliere, "there's one of the leading danseuses whose name on the posters attracts all Paris. That woman earns sixty thousand francs a year and lives like a princess; the price of your manufactory all told wouldn't suffice to buy you the privilege of bidding her good-morning a dozen times."

"Do you see," said Bixiou, "that young man who is sitting on the front seat of her carriage? Well, he's a viscount who bears a fine old name; he's her first gentleman of the bed-chamber; does all her business with the newspapers; carries messages of peace or war in the morning to the director of the Opera; and takes charge of the applause which salutes her as she enters or leaves the stage."

"Well, well, my good friends, that's the finishing touch! I see now that I knew nothing of the ways of Paris."

"At any rate, you are learning what you can see in ten minutes in the Passage de l'Opera," said Bixiou. "Look there."

Two persons, a man and a woman, came out of the Passage at that moment. The woman was neither plain nor pretty; but her dress had that distinction of style and cut and color which reveals an artist; the man had the air of a singer.

"There," said Bixiou, "is a baritone and a second danseuse. The baritone is a man of immense talent, but a baritone voice being only an accessory to the other parts he scarcely earns what the second danseuse earns. The danseuse, who was celebrated before Taglioni and Ellsler appeared, has preserved to our day some of the old traditions of the character dance and pantomime. If the two others had not revealed in the art of dancing a poetry hitherto unperceived, she would have been the leading talent; as it is, she is reduced to the second line. But for all that, she fingers her thirty thousand francs a year, and her faithful friend is a peer of France, very influential in the Chamber. And see! there's a danseuse of the third order, who, as a dancer, exists only through the omnipotence of a newspaper. If her engagement were not renewed the ministry would have one more journalistic enemy on its back. The corps de ballet is a great power; consequently it is considered better form in the upper ranks of dandyism and politics to have relations with dance than with song. In the stalls, where the habitues of the Opera congregate, the saying 'Monsieur is all for singing' is a form of ridicule."

A short man with a common face, quite simply dressed, passed them at this moment.

"There's the other half of the Opera receipts—that man who just went by; the tenor. There is no longer any play, poem, music, or representation of any kind possible unless some celebrated tenor can reach a certain note. The tenor is love, he is the Voice that touches the heart, that vibrates in the soul, and his value is reckoned at a much higher salary than that of a minister. One hundred thousand francs for a throat, one hundred thousand francs for a couple of ankle-bones,—those are the two financial scourges of the Opera."

"I am amazed," said Gazonal, "at the hundreds of thousands of francs walking about here."

"We'll amaze you a good deal more, my dear cousin," said Leon de Lora. "We'll take Paris as an artist takes his violoncello, and show you how it is played,—in short, how people amuse themselves in Paris."

"It is a kaleidoscope with a circumference of twenty miles," cried Gazonal.

"Before piloting monsieur about, I have to see Gaillard," said Bixiou.

"But we can use Gaillard for the cousin," replied Leon.

"What sort of machine is that?" asked Gazonal.

"He isn't a machine, he is a machinist. Gaillard is a friend of ours who has ended a miscellaneous career by becoming the editor of a newspaper, and whose character and finances are governed by movements comparable to those of the tides. Gaillard can contribute to make you win your lawsuit—"

"It is lost."

"That's the very moment to win it," replied Bixiou.

When they reached Theodore Gaillard's abode, which was now in the rue de Menars, the valet ushered the three friends into a boudoir and asked them to wait, as monsieur was in secret conference.

"With whom?" asked Bixiou.

"With a man who is selling him the incarceration of an *unseizable* debtor," replied a handsome woman who now appeared in a charming morning toilet.

"In that case, my dear Suzanne," said Bixiou, "I am certain we may go in."

"Oh! what a beautiful creature!" said Gazonal.

"That is Madame Gaillard," replied Leon de Lora, speaking low into his cousin's ear. "She is the most humble-minded woman in Paris, for she had the public and has contented herself with a husband."

"What is your will, messeigneurs?" said the facetious editor, seeing his two friends and imitating Frederic Lemaitre.

Theodore Gaillard, formerly a wit, had ended by becoming a stupid man in consequence of remaining constantly in one centre,—a moral phenomenon frequently to be observed in Paris. His principal method of conversation consisted in sowing his speeches with sayings taken from plays then in vogue and pronounced in imitation of well-known actors.

"We have come to blague," said Leon.

"'Again, young men'" (Odry in the Saltimbauques).

"Well, this time, we've got him, sure," said Gaillard's other visitor, apparently by way of conclusion.

"*Are* you sure of it, pere Fromenteau?" asked Gaillard. "This it the eleventh time you've caught him at night and missed him in the morning."

"How could I help it? I never saw such a debtor! he's a locomotive; goes to sleep in Paris and wakes up in the Seine-et-Oise. A safety lock I call him." Seeing a smile on Gaillard's face he added: "That's a saying in our business. Pinch a man, means arrest him, lock him up. The criminal police have another term. Vidoeq said to his man, 'You are served'; that's funnier, for it means the guillotine."

A nudge from Bixiou made Gazonal all eyes and ears.

"Does monsieur grease my paws?" asked Fromenteau of Gaillard, in a threatening but cool tone.

"'A question that of fifty centimes'" (Les Saltimbauques), replied the editor, taking out five francs and offering them to Fromenteau.

"And the rapscallions?" said the man.

"What rapscallions?" asked Gaillard.

"Those I employ," replied Fromenteau calmly.

"Is there a lower depth still?" asked Bixiou.

"Yes, monsieur," said the spy. "Some people give us information without knowing they do so, and without getting paid for it. I put fools and ninnies below rapscallions."

"They are often original, and witty, your rapscallions!" said Leon.

"Do you belong to the police?" asked Gazonal, eying with uneasy curiosity the hard, impassible little man, who was dressed like the third clerk in a sheriff's office.

"Which police do you mean?" asked Fromenteau.

"There are several?"

"As many as five," replied the man. "Criminal, the head of which was Vidoeq; secret police, which keeps an eye on the other police, the head of it being always unknown; political police,—that's Fouche's. Then there's the police of Foreign Affairs, and finally, the palace police (of the Emperor, Louis XVIII., etc.), always squabbling with that of the quai Malaquais. It came to an end under Monsieur Decazes. I belonged to the police of Louis XVIII.; I'd been in it since 1793, with that poor Contenson."

The four gentlemen looked at each other with one thought: "How many heads he must have brought to the scaffold!"

"Now-a-days, they are trying to get on without us. Folly!" continued the little man, who began to seem terrible. "Since 1830 they want honest men at the prefecture! I resigned, and I've made myself a small vocation by arresting for debt."

"He is the right arm of the commercial police," said Gaillard in Bixiou's ear, "but you can never find out who pays him most, the debtor or the creditor."

"The more rascally a business is, the more honor it needs. I'm for him who pays me best," continued Fromenteau addressing Gaillard. "You want to recover fifty thousand francs and you talk farthings to your means of action. Give me five hundred francs and your man is pinched to-night, for we spotted him yesterday!"

"Five hundred francs for you alone!" cried Theodore Gaillard.

"Lizette wants a shawl," said the spy, not a muscle of his face moving. "I call her Lizette because of Beranger."

"You have a Lizette, and you stay in such a business!" cried the virtuous Gazonal.

"It is amusing! People may cry up the pleasures of hunting and fishing as much as they like but to stalk a man in Paris is far better fun."

"Certainly," said Gazonal, reflectively, speaking to himself, "they must have great talent."

"If I were to enumerate the qualities which make a man remarkable in our vocation," said Fromenteau, whose rapid glance had enabled him to fathom Gazonal completely, "you'd think I was talking of a man of genius. First, we must have the eyes of a lynx; next, audacity (to tear into houses like bombs, accost the servants as if we knew them, and propose treachery—always agreed to); next, memory, sagacity, invention (to make schemes, conceived rapidly, never the same—for spying must be guided by the characters and habits of the persons spied upon; it is a gift of heaven); and, finally, agility, vigor. All these facilities and qualities, monsieur, are depicted on the door of the Gymnase-Amoros as Virtue. Well, we must have them all, under pain of losing the salaries given us by the State, the rue de Jerusalem, or the minister of Commerce."

"You certainly seem to me a remarkable man," said Gazonal.

Fromenteau looked at the provincial without replying, without betraying the smallest sign of feeling, and departed, bowing to no one,—a trait of real genius.

"Well, cousin, you have now seen the police incarnate," said Leon to Gazonal.

123

"It has something the effect of a dinner-pill," said the worthy provincial, while Gaillard and Bixiou were talking together in a low voice.

"I'll give you an answer to-night at Carabine's," said Gaillard aloud, re-seating himself at his desk without seeing or bowing to Gazonal.

"He is a rude fellow!" cried the Southerner as they left the room.

"His paper has twenty-two thousand subscribers," said Leon de Lora. "He is one of the five great powers of the day, and he hasn't, in the morning, the time to be polite. Now," continued Leon, speaking to Bixiou, "if we are going to the Chamber to help him with his lawsuit let us take the longest way round."

"Words said by great men are like silver-gilt spoons with the gilt washed off; by dint of repetition they lose their brilliancy," said Bixiou. "Where shall we go?"

"Here, close by, to our hatter?" replied Leon.

"Bravo!" cried Bixiou. "If we keep on in this way, we shall have an amusing day of it."

"Gazonal," said Leon, "I shall make the man pose for you; but mind that you keep a serious face, like the king on a five-franc piece, for you are going to see a choice original, a man whose importance has turned his head. In these days, my dear fellow, under our new political dispensation, every human being tries to cover himself with glory, and most of them cover themselves with ridicule; hence a lot of living caricatures quite new to the world."

"If everybody gets glory, who can be famous?" said Gazonal.

"Fame! none but fools want that," replied Bixiou. "Your cousin wears the cross, but I'm the better dressed of the two, and it is I whom people are looking at."

After this remark, which may explain why orators and other great statesmen no longer put the ribbon in their buttonholes when in Paris, Leon showed Gazonal a sign, bearing, in golden letters, the illustrious name of "Vital, successor to Finot, manufacturer of hats" (no longer "hatter" as formerly), whose advertisements brought in more money to the newspapers than those of any half-dozen vendors of pills or sugarplums,—the author, moreover, of an essay on hats.

"My dear fellow," said Bixiou to Gazonal, pointing to the splendors of the show-window, "Vital has forty thousand francs a year from invested property."

"And he stays a hatter!" cried the Southerner, with a bound that almost broke the arm which Bixiou had linked in his.

"You shall see the man," said Leon. "You need a hat and you shall have one gratis."

"Is Monsieur Vital absent?" asked Bixiou, seeing no one behind the desk.

"Monsieur is correcting proof in his study," replied the head clerk.

"Hein! what style!" said Leon to his cousin; then he added, addressing the clerk: "Could we speak to him without injury to his inspiration?"

"Let those gentlemen enter," said a voice.

It was a bourgeois voice, the voice of one eligible to the Chamber, a powerful voice, a wealthy voice.

Vital deigned to show himself, dressed entirely in black cloth, with a splendid frilled shirt adorned with one diamond. The three friends observed a young and pretty woman sitting near the desk, working at some embroidery.

Vital is a man between thirty and forty years of age, with a natural joviality now repressed by ambitious ideas. He is blessed with that medium height which is the privilege of sound organizations. He is rather plump, and takes great pains with his person. His forehead is getting bald, but he uses that circumstance to give himself the air of a man consumed by thought. It is easy to see by the way his wife looks at him and listens to him that she believes in the genius and glory of her husband. Vital loves artists, not that he has any taste for art, but from fellowship; for he feels himself an artist, and makes this felt by disclaiming that title of nobility, and placing himself with constant premeditation at so great a distance from the arts that persons may be forced to say to him: "You have raised the construction of hats to the height of a science."

"Have you at last discovered a hat to suit me?" asked Leon de Lora.

"Why, monsieur! in fifteen days?" replied Vital, "and for you! Two months would hardly suffice to invent a shape in keeping with your countenance. See, here is your lithographic portrait: I have studied it most carefully. I would not give myself that trouble for a prince; but you are more; you are an artist, and you understand me."

"This is one of our greatest inventors," said Bixiou presenting Gazonal. "He might be as great as Jacquart if he would only let himself die. Our friend, a manufacturer of cloth, has discovered a method of replacing the indigo in old blue coats, and he wants to see you as another great phenomenon, because he has heard of your saying, 'The hat is the man.' That speech of yours enraptured him. Ah! Vital, you have faith; you believe in something; you have enthusiasm for your work."

Vital scarcely listened; he grew pale with pleasure.

"Rise, my wife! Monsieur is a man of science."

Madame Vital rose at her husband's gesture. Gazonal bowed to her.

"Shall I have the honor to cover your head?" said Vital, with joyful obsequiousness.

"At the same price as mine," interposed Bixiou.

"Of course, of course; I ask no other fee than to be quoted by you, messieurs—Monsieur needs a picturesque hat, something in the style of Monsieur Lousteau's," he continued, looking at Gazonal with the eye of a master. "I will consider it."

"You give yourself a great deal of trouble," said Gazonal.

"Oh! for a few persons only; for those who know how to appreciate the value of the pains I bestow upon them. Now, take the aristocracy—there is but one man there who has truly comprehended the Hat; and that is the Prince de Bethune. How is it that men do not consider, as women do, that the hat is the first thing that strikes the eye? And why have they never thought of changing the present system, which is, let us say it frankly, ignoble? Yes, ignoble; and yet a Frenchman is, of all nationalities, the one most persistent in this folly! I know the difficulties of a change, messieurs. I don't speak of my own writings on the matter, which, as I think, approach it philosophically, but simply as a hatter. I have myself studied means to accentuate the infamous head-covering to which France is now enslaved until I succeed in overthrowing it."

So saying he pointed to the hideous hat in vogue at the present day.

"Behold the enemy, messieurs," he continued. "How is it that the wittiest and most satirical people on earth will consent to wear upon their heads a bit of stove-pipe?—as one of our great writers has called it. Here are some of the infections I have been able to give to those atrocious lines," he added, pointing to a number of his creations. "But, although I am able to conform them to the character of each wearer—for, as you see, there are the hats of a doctor, a grocer, a dandy, an artist, a fat man, a thin man, and so forth—the style itself remains horrible. Seize, I beg of you, my whole thought—"

He took up a hat, low-crowned and wide-brimmed.

"This," he continued, "is the old hat of Claude Vignon, a great critic, in the days when he was a free man and a free-liver. He has lately come round to the ministry; they've made him a professor, a librarian; he writes now for the Debats only; they've appointed him Master of Petitions with a salary of sixteen thousand francs; he earns four thousand more out of his paper, and he is decorated. Well, now see his new hat."

And Vital showed them a hat of a form and design which was truly expressive of the juste-milieu.

"You ought to have made him a Punch and Judy hat!" cried Gazonal.

"You are a man of genius, Monsieur Vital," said Leon.

Vital bowed.

"Would you kindly tell me why the shops of your trade in Paris remain open late at night,—later than the cafes and the wineshops? That fact puzzles me very much," said Gazonal.

"In the first place, our shops are much finer when lighted up than they are in the daytime; next, where we sell ten hats in the daytime we sell fifty at night."

"Everything is queer in Paris," said Leon.

"Thanks to my efforts and my successes," said Vital, returning to the course of his self-laudation, "we are coming to hats with round headpieces. It is to that I tend!"

"What obstacle is there?" asked Gazonal.

"Cheapness, monsieur. In the first place, very handsome silk hats can be built for fifteen francs, which kills our business; for in Paris no one ever has fifteen francs in his pocket to spend on a hat. If a beaver hat costs thirty, it is still the same thing—When I say beaver, I ought to state that there are not ten pounds of beaver skins left in France. That article is worth three hundred and fifty francs a pound, and it takes an ounce for a hat. Besides, a beaver hat isn't really worth anything; the skin takes a wretched dye; gets rusty in ten minutes under the sun, and heat puts it out of shape as well. What we call 'beaver' in the trade is neither more nor less than hare's-skin. The best qualities are made from the back of the animal, the second from the sides, the third from the belly. I confide to you these trade secrets because you are men of honor. But whether a man has hare's-skin or silk on his head, fifteen or thirty francs in short, the problem is always insoluble. Hats must be paid for in cash, and that is why the hat remains what it is. The honor of vestural France will be saved on the day that gray hats with round crowns can be made to cost a hundred francs. We could then, like the tailors, give credit. To reach that result men must resolve to wear buckles, gold lace, plumes, and the brims lined with satin, as in the days of Louis XIII. and Louis XIV. Our business, which would then enter the domain of fancy, would increase tenfold. The markets of the world should belong to France; Paris will forever give the tone to women's fashions, and yet the hats which all Frenchmen wear to-day are made in every country on earth! There are ten millions of foreign money to be gained annually for France in that question—"

"A revolution!" cried Bixiou, pretending enthusiasm.

"Yes, and a radical one; for the form must be changed."

"You are happy after the manner of Luther in dreaming of reform," said Leon.

"Yes, monsieur. Ah! if a dozen or fifteen artists, capitalists, or dandies who set the tone would only have courage for twenty-four hours France would gain a splendid commercial battle! To succeed in this reform I would give my whole fortune! Yes, my sole ambition is to regenerate the hat and disappear."

"The man is colossal," said Gazonal, as they left the shop; "but I assure you that all your originals so far have a touch of the Southerner about them."

"Let us go this way," said Bixiou pointing to the rue Saint-Marc.

"Do you want to show me something else?"

"Yes; you shall see the usuress of rats, marcheuses and great ladies,—a woman who possesses more terrible secrets than there are gowns hanging in her window," said Bixiou.

And he showed Gazonal one of those untidy shops which made an ugly stain in the midst of the dazzling show-windows of modern retail commerce. This shop had a front painted in 1820, which some bankrupt had doubtless left in a dilapidated condition. The color had disappeared beneath a double coating of dirt, the result of usage, and a thick layer of dust; the window-panes were filthy, the door-knob turned of itself, as door-knobs do in all places where people go out more quickly than they enter.

"What do you say of *that*? First cousin to Death, isn't she?" said Leon in Gazonal's ear, showing him, at the desk, a terrible individual. "Well, she calls herself Madame Nourrisson."

"Madame, how much is this guipure?" asked the manufacturer, intending to compete in liveliness with the two artists.

"To you, monsieur, who come from the country, it will be only three hundred francs," she replied. Then, remarking in his manner a sort of eagerness peculiar to Southerners, she added, in a grieved tone, "It formerly belonged to that poor Princess de Lamballe."

"What! do you dare exhibit it so near the palace?" cried Bixiou.

"Monsieur, *they* don't believe in it," she replied.

"Madame, we have not come to make purchases," said Bixiou, with a show of frankness.

"So I see, monsieur," returned Madame Nourrisson.

"We have several things to sell," said the illustrious caricaturist. "I live close by, rue de Richelieu, 112, sixth floor. If you will come round there for a moment, you may perhaps make some good bargains."

Ten minutes later Madame Nourrisson did in fact present herself at Bixiou's lodgings, where by that time he had taken Leon and Gazonal. Madame Nourrisson found them all three as serious as authors whose collaboration does not meet with the success it deserves.

"Madame," said the intrepid hoaxer, showing her a pair of women's slippers, "these belonged formerly to the Empress Josephine."

He felt it incumbent on him to return change for the Prince de Lamballe.

"Those!" she exclaimed; "they were made this year; look at the mark."

"Don't you perceive that the slippers are only by way of preface?" said Leon; "though, to be sure, they are usually the conclusion of a tale."

"My friend here," said Bixiou, motioning to Gazonal, "has an immense family interest in ascertaining whether a young lady of a good and wealthy house, whom he wishes to marry, has ever gone wrong."

"How much will monsieur give for the information," she asked, looking at Gazonal, who was no longer surprised by anything.

"One hundred francs," he said.

"No, thank you!" she said with a grimace of refusal worthy of a macaw.

"Then say how much you want, my little Madame Nourrisson," cried Bixiou catching her round the waist.

"In the first place, my dear gentlemen, I have never, since I've been in the business, found man or woman to haggle over happiness. Besides," she said, letting a cold smile flicker on her lips, and enforcing it by an icy glance full of catlike distrust, "if it doesn't concern your happiness, it concerns your fortune; and at the height where I find you lodging no man haggles over a 'dot'—Come," she said, "out with it! What is it you want to know, my lambs?"

"About the Beunier family," replied Bixiou, very glad to find out something in this indirect manner about persons in whom he was interested.

"Oh! as for that," she said, "one louis is quite enough."

"Why?"

"Because I hold all the mother's jewels and she's on tenter-hooks every three months, I can tell you! It is hard work for her to pay the interest on what I've lent her. Do you want to marry there, simpleton?" she added, addressing Gazonal; "then pay me forty francs and I'll talk four hundred worth."

Gazonal produced a forty-franc gold-piece, and Madame Nourrisson gave him startling details as to the secret penury of certain so-called fashionable women. This dealer in cast-off clothes, getting lively as she talked, pictured herself unconsciously while telling of others. Without betraying a single name or any secret, she made the three men shudder by proving to them how little so-called happiness existed in Paris that did not rest on the vacillating foundation of borrowed money. She possessed, laid away in her drawers, the secrets of departed grandmothers, living children, deceased husbands, dead granddaughters,—memories set in gold and diamonds. She learned appalling stories by making her clients talk of one another; tearing their secrets from them in moments of passion, of quarrels, of anger, and during those cooler negotiations which need a loan to settle difficulties.

"Why were you ever induced to take up such a business?" asked Gazonal.

"For my son's sake," she said naively.

Such women almost invariably justify their trade by alleging noble motives. Madame Nourrisson posed as having lost several opportunities for marriage, also three daughters who had gone to the bad, and all her illusions. She showed the pawn-tickets of the Mont-de-Piete to prove the risks her business ran; declared that she did not know how to meet the "end of the month"; she was robbed, she said,—*robbed.*

The two artists looked at each other on hearing that expression, which seemed exaggerated.

"Look here, my sons, I'll show you how we are *done*. It is not about myself, but about my opposite neighbour, Madame Mahuchet, a ladies' shoemaker. I had loaned money to a countess, a woman who has too many passions for her means,—lives in a fine apartment filled with splendid furniture, and makes, as we say, a devil of a show with her high and mighty airs. She owed three hundred francs to her shoemaker, and was giving a dinner no later than yesterday. The shoemaker, who heard of the dinner from the cook, came to see me; we got excited, and she wanted to make a row; but I said: 'My dear Madame Mahuchet, what good will that do? you'll only get yourself hated. It is much better to obtain some security; and you save your bile.' She wouldn't listen, but go she would, and asked me to support her; so I went. 'Madame is not at home.'—'Up to that! we'll wait,' said Madame Mahuchet, 'if we have to stay all night,'—and down we camped in the antechamber. Presently the doors began to open and shut, and feet and voices came along. I felt badly. The guests were arriving for dinner. You can see the appearance it had. The countess sent her maid to coax Madame Mahuchet: 'Pay you to-morrow!' in short, all the snares! Nothing took. The countess, dressed to the nines, went to the dining-room. Mahuchet heard her and opened the door. Gracious! when she saw that table sparkling with silver, the covers to the dishes and the chandeliers all glittering like a jewel-case, didn't she go off like soda-water and fire her shot: 'When people spend the money of others they should be sober and not give dinner-parties. Think of your being a countess and owing three hundred francs to a poor shoemaker with seven children!' You can guess how she railed, for the Mahuchet hasn't any education. When the countess tried to make an excuse ('no money') Mahuchet screamed out: 'Look at all your fine silver, madame; pawn it and pay me!'—'Take some yourself,' said the countess quickly, gathering up a quantity of forks and spoons and putting them into her hands. Downstairs we rattled!—heavens! like success itself. No, before we got to the street Mahuchet began to cry—she's a kind woman! She turned back and restored the silver; for she now understood that countess' poverty—it was plated ware!"

"And she forked it over," said Leon, in whom the former Mistigris occasionally reappeared.

"Ah! my dear monsieur," said Madame Nourrisson, enlightened by the slang, "you are an artist, you write plays, you live in the rue du Helder and are friends with Madame Anatolia; you have habits that I know all about. Come, do you want some rarity in the grand style,—Carabine or Mousqueton, Malaga or Jenny Cadine?"

"Malaga, Carabine! nonsense!" cried Leon de Lora. "It was we who invented them."

"I assure you, my good Madame Nourrisson," said Bixiou, "that we only wanted the pleasure of making your acquaintance, and we should like very much to be informed as to how you ever came to slip into this business."

"I was confidential maid in the family of a marshal of France, Prince d'Ysembourg," she said, assuming the airs of a Dorine. "One morning, one of the most beplumed countesses of the Imperial court came to the house and wanted to speak to the marshal privately. I put myself in the way of hearing what she said. She burst into tears and confided to that booby of a marshal—yes, the Conde of the Republic is a booby!—that her husband, who served under him in Spain, had left her without means, and if she didn't get a thousand francs, or two thousand, that day her children must go without food; she hadn't any for the morrow. The marshal, who was always ready to give in those days, took two notes of a thousand francs each out of his desk, and gave them to her. I saw that fine countess going down the staircase where she couldn't see me. She was laughing with a satisfaction that certainly wasn't motherly, so I slipped after her to the peristyle where I heard her say to the coachman, 'To Leroy's.' I ran round quickly to Leroy's, and there, sure enough, was the poor mother. I got there in time to see her order and pay for a fifteen-hundred-franc dress; you understand that in those days people were made to pay when they bought. The next day but one she appeared at an ambassador's ball, dressed to please all the world and some one in particular. That day I said to myself: 'I've got a career! When I'm no longer young I'll lend money to great ladies on their finery; for passion never calculates, it pays blindly.' If you want subjects for a vaudeville I can sell you plenty."

She departed after delivering this tirade, in which all the phases of her past life were outlined, leaving Gazonal as much horrified by her revelations as by the five yellow teeth she showed when she tried to smile.

"What shall we do now?" he asked presently.

"Make notes," replied Bixiou, whistling for his porter; "for I want some money, and I'll show you the use of porters. You think they only pull the gate-cord; whereas they really pull poor devils like me and artists whom they take under their protection out of difficulties. Mine will get the Montyon prize one of these days."

Gazonal opened his eyes to their utmost roundness.

A man between two ages, partly a graybeard, partly an office-boy, but more oily within and without, hair greasy, stomach puffy, skin dull and moist, like that of the prior of a convent, always wearing list shoes, a blue coat, and grayish trousers, made his appearance.

"What is it, monsieur?" he said with an air which combined that of a protector and a subordinate.

"Ravenouillet—His name is Ravenouillet," said Bixiou turning to Gazonal. "Have you our notebook of bills due with you?"

Ravenouillet pulled out of his pocket the greasiest and stickiest book that Gazonal's eyes had ever beheld.

"Write down at three months' sight two notes of five hundred francs each, which you will proceed to sign."

And Bixiou handed over two notes already drawn to his order by Ravenouillet, which Ravenouillet immediately signed and inscribed on the greasy book, in which his wife also kept account of the debts of the other lodgers.

"Thanks, Ravenouillet," said Bixiou. "And here's a box at the Vaudeville for you."

"Oh! my daughter will enjoy that," said Ravenouillet, departing.

"There are seventy-one tenants in this house," said Bixiou, "and the average of what they owe Ravenouillet is six thousand francs a month, eighteen thousand quarterly for money advanced, postage, etc., not counting the rents due. He is Providence—at thirty per cent, which we all pay him, though he never asks for anything."

"Oh, Paris! Paris!" cried Gazonal.

"I'm going to take you now, cousin Gazonal," said Bixiou, after indorsing the notes, "to see another comedian, who will play you a charming scene gratis."

"Who is it?" said Gazonal.

"A usurer. As we go along I'll tell you the debut of friend Ravenouillet in Paris."

Passing in front of the porter's lodge, Gazonal saw Mademoiselle Lucienne Ravenouillet holding in her hand a music score (she was a pupil of the

Conservatoire), her father reading a newspaper, and Madame Ravenouillet with a package of letters to be carried up to the lodgers.

"Thanks, Monsieur Bixiou!" said the girl.

"She's not a rat," explained Leon to his cousin; "she is the larva of the grasshopper."

"Here's the history of Ravenouillet," continued Bixiou, when the three friends reached the boulevard. "In 1831 Massol, the councillor of state who is dealing with your case, was a lawyer-journalist who at that time never thought of being more than Keeper of the Seals, and deigned to have King Louis-Philippe on his throne. Forgive his ambition, he's from Carcassonne. One morning there entered to him a young rustic of his parts, who said: 'You know me very well, Mossoo Massol; I'm your neighbour the grocer's little boy; I've come from down there, for they tell me a fellow is certain to get a place if he comes to Paris.' Hearing these words, Massol shuddered, and said to himself that if he were weak enough to help this compatriot (to him utterly unknown) he should have the whole department prone upon him, his bell-rope would break, his valet leave him, he should have difficulties with his landlord about the stairway, and the other lodgers would assuredly complain of the smell of garlic pervading the house. Consequently, he looked at his visitor as a butcher looks at a sheep whose throat he intends to cut. But whether the rustic comprehended the stab of that glance or not, he went on to say (so Massol told me), 'I've as much ambition as other men. I will never go back to my native place, if I ever do go back, unless I am a rich man. Paris is the antechamber of Paradise. They tell me that you who write the newspapers can make, as they say, 'fine weather and foul'; that is, you have things all your own way, and it's enough to ask your help to get any place, no matter what, under government. Now, though I have faculties, like others, I know myself: I have no education; I don't know how to write, and that's a misfortune, for I have ideas. I am not seeking, therefore, to be your rival; I judge myself, and I know I couldn't succeed there. But, as you are so powerful, and as we are almost brothers, having played together in childhood, I count upon you to launch me in a career and to protect me—Oh, you *must*; I want a place, a place suitable to my capacity, to such as I am, a place were I can make my fortune.' Massol was just about to put his compatriot neck and crop out of the door with some brutal speech, when the rustic ended his appeal thus: 'I don't ask to enter the administration where people advance like tortoises—there's your cousin, who has stuck in one post for twenty years. No, I only want to make my debut.'—'On the stage?' asked Massol only too happy at that conclusion.—'No, though I have gesture enough, and figure, and memory. But there's too much wear and tear; I prefer the career of *porter.*' Massol kept his countenance, and replied: 'I think there's more wear and tear in that, but as your choice is made I'll see what I can do'; and he got him, as Ravenouillet says, his first 'cordon.'"

"I was the first master," said Leon, "to consider the race of porter. You'll find knaves of morality, mountebanks of vanity, modern sycophants, septembriseurs, disguised in philanthropy, inventors of palpitating questions, preaching the emancipation of the negroes, improvement of little thieves, benevolence to liberated convicts, and who, nevertheless, leave their porters in a condition worse than that of the Irish, in holes more dreadful than a mud cabin, and pay them less money to live on than the State pays to support a convict. I have done but one good action in my life, and that was to build my porter a decent lodge."

"Yes," said Bixiou, "if a man, having built a great cage divided into thousands of compartments like the cells of a beehive or the dens of a menagerie, constructed to receive human beings of all trades and all kinds, if that animal, calling itself the proprietor, should go to a man of science and say: 'I want an individual of the bimanous species, able to live in holes full of old boots, pestiferous with rags, and ten feet square; I want him such that he can live there all his life, sleep there, eat there, be happy, get children as pretty as little cupids, work, toil, cultivate flowers, sing there, stay there, and live in darkness but see and know everything,' most assuredly the man of science could never have invented the porter to oblige the proprietor; Paris, and Paris only could create him, or, if you choose, the devil."

"Parisian creative powers have gone farther than that," said Gazonal; "look at the workmen! You don't know all the products of industry, though you exhibit them. Our toilers fight against the toilers of the continent by force of misery, as Napoleon fought Europe by force of regiments."

"Here we are, at my friend the usurer's," said Bixiou. "His name is Vauvinet. One of the greatest mistakes made by writers who describe our manners and morals is to harp on old portraits. In these days all trades change. The grocer becomes a peer of France, artists capitalize their money, vaudevillists have incomes. A few rare beings may remain what they originally were, but professions in general have no longer either their special costume or their formerly fixed habits and ways. In the past we had Gobseck, Gigounet, Samonon,—the last of the Romans; to-day we rejoice in Vauvinet, the good-fellow usurer, the dandy who frequents the greenroom and the lorettes, and drives about in a little coupe with one horse. Take special note of my man, friend Gazonal, and you'll see the comedy of money, the cold man who won't give a penny, the hot man who snuffs a profit; listen to him attentively!"

All three went up to the second floor of a fine-looking house on the boulevard des Italiens, where they found themselves surrounded by the elegances then in fashion. A young man about twenty-eight years of age advanced to meet them with a smiling face, for he saw Leon de Lora first. Vauvinet held out his hand with apparent friendliness to Bixiou, and bowed coldly to Gazonal as he motioned them to enter his office, where bourgeois taste was visible beneath the artistic appearance of the furniture, and in spite of the statuettes and the thousand other little trifles applied to our little apartments by modern art, which has made itself as small as its patrons.

Vauvinet was dressed, like other young men of our day who go into business, with extreme elegance, which many of them regard as a species of prospectus.

"I've come for some money," said Bixiou, laughing, and presenting his notes.

Vauvinet assumed a serious air, which made Gazonal smile, such difference was there between the smiling visage that received them and the countenance of the money-lender recalled to business.

"My dear fellow," said Vauvinet, looking at Bixiou, "I should certainly oblige you with the greatest pleasure, but I haven't any money to loan at the present time."

"Ah, bah!"

"No; I have given all I had to—you know who. That poor Lousteau went into partnership for the management of a theatre with an old vaudevillist who has great influence with the ministry, Ridal; and they came to me yesterday for thirty thousand francs. I'm cleaned out, and so completely that I was just in the act of sending to Cerizet for a hundred louis, when I lost at lansquenet this morning, at Jenny Cadine's."

"You must indeed me hard-up if you can't oblige this poor Bixiou," said Leon de Lora; "for he can be very sharp-tongued when he hasn't a sou."

"Well," said Bixiou, "I could never say anything but good of Vauvinet; he's full of goods."

"My dear friend," said Vauvinet, "if I had the money, I couldn't possibly discount, even at fifty per cent, notes which are drawn by your porter. Ravenouillet's paper isn't in demand. He's not a Rothschild. I warn you that his notes are worn thin; you had better invent another firm. Find an uncle. As for a friend who'll sign notes for us there's no such being to be found; the matter-of-factness of the present age is making awful progress."

"I have a friend," said Bixiou, motioning to Leon's cousin. "Monsieur here; one of the most distinguished manufacturers of cloth in the South, named Gazonal. His hair is not very well dressed," added Bixiou, looking at the touzled and luxuriant crop on the provincial's head, "but I am going to take him to Marius, who will make him look less like a poodle-dog, an appearance so injurious to his credit, and to ours."

"I don't believe in Southern securities, be it said without offence to monsieur," replied Vauvinet, with whom Gazonal was so entertained that he did not resent his insolence.

Gazonal, that extremely penetrating intellect, thought that the painter and Bixiou intended, by way of teaching him to know Paris, to make him pay the thousand francs for his breakfast at the Cafe de Paris, for this son of the Pyrenees had never got out of that armor of distrust which incloses the provincial in Paris.

"How can you expect me to have outstanding business at seven hundred miles from Paris?" added Vauvinet.

"Then you refuse me positively?" asked Bixiou.

"I have twenty francs, and no more," said the young usurer.

"I'm sorry for you," said the joker. "I thought I was worth a thousand francs."

"You are worth two hundred thousand francs," replied Vauvinet, "and sometimes you are worth your weight in gold, or at least your tongue is; but I tell you I haven't a penny."

"Very good," replied Bixiou; "then we won't say anything more about it. I had arranged for this evening, at Carabine's, the thing you most wanted—you know?"

Vauvinet winked an eye at Bixiou; the wink that two jockeys give each other when they want to say: "Don't try trickery."

"Don't you remember catching me round the waist as if I were a pretty woman," said Bixiou, "and coaxing me with look and speech, and saying, 'I'll do anything for you if you'll only get me shares at par in that railroad du Tillet and Nucingen have made an offer for?' Well, old fellow, du Tillet and Nucingen are coming to Carabine's to-night, where they will meet a number of political characters. You've lost a fine opportunity. Good-bye to you, old carrot."

Bixiou rose, leaving Vauvinet apparently indifferent, but inwardly annoyed by the sense that he had committed a folly.

"One moment, my dear fellow," said the money-lender. "Though I haven't the money, I have credit. If your notes are worth nothing, I can keep them and give you notes in exchange. If we can come to an agreement about that railway stock we could share the profits, of course in due proportion and I'll allow you that on—"

"No, no," said Bixiou, "I want money in hand, and I must get those notes of Ravenouillet's cashed."

"Ravenouillet is sound," said Vauvinet. "He puts money into the savings-bank; he is good security."

"Better than you," interposed Leon, "for HE doesn't stipend lorettes; he hasn't any rent to pay; and he never rushes into speculations which keep him dreading either a rise or fall."

"You think you can laugh at me, great man," returned Vauvinet, once more jovial and caressing; "you've turned La Fontaine's fable of 'Le Chene et le Roseau' into an elixir—Come, Gubetta, my old accomplice," he continued, seizing Bixiou round the waist, "you want money; well, I can borrow three thousand francs from my friend Cerizet instead of two; 'Let us be friends, Cinna!' hand over your colossal cabbages,—made to trick the public like a gardener's catalogue. If I refused you it was because it is pretty hard on a man who can only do his poor little business by turning over his money, to have to keep your Ravenouillet notes in the drawer of his desk. Hard, hard, very hard!"

"What discount do you want?" asked Bixiou.

"Next to nothing," returned Vauvinet. "It will cost you a miserable fifty francs at the end of the quarter."

"As Emile Blondet used to say, you shall be my benefactor," replied Bixiou.

"Twenty per cent!" whispered Gazonal to Bixiou, who replied by a punch of his elbow in the provincial's oesophagus.

"Bless me!" said Vauvinet opening a drawer in his desk as if to put away the Ravenouillet notes, "here's an old bill of five hundred francs stuck in the drawer! I didn't know I was so rich. And here's a note payable at the end of the month for four hundred and fifty; Cerizet will take it without much diminution, and there's your sum in hand. But no nonsense, Bixiou! Hein? to-night, at Carabine's, will you swear to me—"

"Haven't we *re*-friended?" said Bixiou, pocketing the five-hundred-franc bill and the note for four hundred and fifty. "I give you my word of honor that you shall see du Tillet, and many other men who want to make their way—their railway—to-night at Carabine's."

Vauvinet conducted the three friends to the landing of the staircase, cajoling Bixiou on the way. Bixiou kept a grave face till he reached the outer door, listening to Gazonal, who tried to enlighten him on his late operation, and to prove to him that if Vauvinet's follower, Cerizet, took another twenty francs out of his four hundred and fifty, he was getting money at forty per cent.

When they reached the asphalt Bixiou frightened Gazonal by the laugh of a Parisian hoaxer,—that cold, mute laugh, a sort of labial north wind.

"The assignment of the contract for that railway is adjourned, positively, by the Chamber; I heard this yesterday from that marcheuse whom we smiled at just now. If I win five or six thousand francs at lansquenet to-night, why should I grudge sixty-five francs for the power to stake, hey?"

"Lansquenet is another of the thousand facets of Paris as it is," said Leon. "And therefore, cousin, I intend to present you to-night in the salon of a duchess,—a duchess of the rue Saint-Georges, where you will see the aristocracy of the lorettes, and probably be able to win your lawsuit. But it is quite impossible to present you anywhere with that mop of Pyrenean hair; you look like a porcupine; and therefore we'll take you close by, Place de la Bourse, to Marius, another of our comedians—"

"Who is he?"

"I'll tell you his tale," said Bixiou. "In the year 1800 a Toulousian named Cabot, a young wig-maker devoured by ambition, came to Paris, and set up a shop (I use your slang). This man of genius,—he now has an income of twenty-four thousand francs a year, and lives, retired from business, at Libourne,—well, he saw that so vulgar and ignoble a name as Cabot could never attain celebrity. Monsieur de Parny, whose hair he cut, gave him the name of Marius, infinitely superior, you perceive, to the Christian names of Armand and Hippolyte, behind which patronymics attacked by the Cabot evil are wont to hide. All the successors of Cabot have called themselves Marius. The present Marius is Marius V.; his real name is Mongin. This occurs in various other trades; for 'Botot water,' and for 'Little-Virtue' ink. Names become commercial property in Paris, and have ended by constituting a sort of ensign of nobility. The present Marius, who takes pupils, has created, he says, the leading school of hair-dressing in the world.

"I've seen, in coming through France," said Gazonal, "a great many signs bearing the words: 'Such a one, pupil of Marius.'"

"His pupils have to wash their hands after every head," said Bixiou; "but Marius does not take them indifferently; they must have nice hands, and not be ill-looking. The most remarkable for manners, appearance, and elocution are sent out to dress heads; and they come back tired to death. Marius himself never turns out except for titled women; he drives his cabriolet and has a groom."

"But, after all, he is nothing but a barber!" cried Gazonal, somewhat shocked.

"Barber!" exclaimed Bixiou; "please remember that he is captain in the National Guard, and is decorated for being the first to spring into a barricade in 1832."

"And take care what you say to him: he is neither barber, hair-dresser, nor wig-maker; he is a director of salons for hair-dressing," said Leon, as they went up a staircase with crystal balusters and mahogany rail, the steps of which were covered with a sumptuous carpet.

"Ah ca! mind you don't compromise us," said Bixiou. "In the antechamber you'll see lacqueys who will take off your coat, and seize your hat, to brush them; and they'll accompany you to the door of the salons to open and shut it. I mention this, friend Gazonal," added Bixiou, slyly, "lest you might think they were after your property, and cry 'Stop thief!'"

"These salons," said Leon, "are three boudoirs where the director has collected all the inventions of modern luxury: lambrequins to the windows, jardinieres everywhere, downy divans where each customer can wait his turn and read the newspapers. You might suppose, when you first go in, that five francs would be the least they'd get out of your waistcoat pocket; but nothing is ever extracted beyond ten sous for combing and frizzing your hair, or twenty sous for cutting and frizzing. Elegant dressing-tables stand about among the jardinieres; water is laid on to the washstands; enormous mirrors reproduce the whole figure. Therefore don't look astonished. When the client (that's the elegant word substituted by Marius for the ignoble word customer),—when the client appears at the door, Marius gives him a glance which appraises him: to Marius you are a *head*, more or less susceptible of occupying his mind. To him there's no mankind; there are only heads."

"We let you hear Marius on all the notes of his scale," said Bixiou, "and you know how to follow our lead."

As soon as Gazonal showed himself, the glance was given, and was evidently favourable, for Marius exclaimed: "Regulus! yours this head! Prepare it first with the little scissors."

"Excuse me," said Gazonal to the pupil, at a sign from Bixiou. "I prefer to have my head dressed by Monsieur Marius himself."

Marius, much flattered by this demand, advanced, leaving the head on which he was engaged.

"I am with you in a moment; I am just finishing. Pray have no uneasiness, my pupil will prepare you; I alone will decide the cut."

Marius, a slim little man, his hair frizzed like that of Rubini, and jet black, dressed also in black, with long white cuffs, and the frill of his shirt adorned with a diamond, now saw Bixiou, to whom he bowed as to a power the equal of his own.

"That is only an ordinary head," he said to Leon, pointing to the person on whom he was operating,—"a grocer, or something of that kind. But if we devoted ourselves to art only, we should lie in Bicetre, mad!" and he turned back with an inimitable gesture to his client, after saying to Regulus, "Prepare monsieur, he is evidently an artist."

"A journalist," said Bixiou.

Hearing that word, Marius gave two or three strokes of the comb to the ordinary head and flung himself upon Gazonal, taking Regulus by the arm at the instant that the pupil was about to begin the operation of the little scissors.

"I will take charge of monsieur. Look, monsieur," he said to the grocer, "reflect yourself in the great mirror—if the mirror permits. Ossian!"

A lacquey entered, and took hold of the client to dress him.

"You pay at the desk, monsieur," said Marius to the stupefied grocer, who was pulling out his purse.

"Is there any use, my dear fellow," said Bixiou, "in going through this operation of the little scissors?"

"No head ever comes to me uncleansed," replied the illustrious hair-dresser; "but for your sake, I will do that of monsieur myself, wholly. My pupils sketch out the scheme, or my strength would not hold out. Every one says as you do: 'Dressed by Marius!' Therefore, I can give only the finishing strokes. What journal is monsieur on?"

"If I were you, I should keep three or four Mariuses," said Gazonal.

"Ah! monsieur, I see, is a feuilletonist," said Marius. "Alas! in dressing heads which expose us to notice it is impossible. Excuse me!"

He left Gazonal to overlook Regulus, who was "preparing" a newly arrived head. Tapping his tongue against his palate, he made a disapproving noise, which may perhaps be written down as "titt, titt, titt."

"There, there! good heavens! that cut is not square; your scissors are hacking it. Here! see there! Regulus, you are not clipping poodles; these are men—who have a character; if you continue to look at the ceiling instead of looking only between the glass and the head, you will dishonor my house."

"You are stern, Monsieur Marius."

"I owe them the secrets of my art."

"Then it is an art?" said Gazonal.

Marius, affronted, looked at Gazonal in the glass, and stopped short, the scissors in one hand, the comb in the other.

"Monsieur, you speak like a—child! and yet, from your accent, I judge you are from the South, the birthplace of men of genius."

"Yes, I know that hair-dressing requires some taste," replied Gazonal.

"Hush, monsieur, hush! I expected better things of YOU. Let me tell you that a hair-dresser,—I don't say a good hair-dresser, for a man is, or he is not, a hair-dresser,—a hair-dresser, I repeat, is more difficult to find than—what shall I say? than—I don't know what—a minister?—(Sit still!) No, for you can't judge by ministers, the streets are full of them. A Paganini? No, he's not great enough. A hair-dresser, monsieur, a man who divines your soul and your habits, in order to dress your hair conformably with your being, that man has all that constitutes a philosopher—and such he is. See the women! Women appreciate us; they know our value; our value to them is the conquest they make when they have placed their heads in our hands to attain a triumph. I say to you that a hair-dresser—the world does not know what he is. I who speak to you, I am very nearly all that there is of—without boasting I may say I am known—Still, I think more might be done—The execution, that is everything! Ah! if women would only give me carte blanche!—if I might only execute the ideas that come to me! I have, you see, a hell of imagination!—but the women don't fall in with it; they have their own plans; they'll stick their fingers or combs, as soon as my back is turned, through the most delicious edifices—which ought to be engraved and perpetuated; for our works, monsieur, last unfortunately but a few hours. A great hair-dresser, hey! he's like Careme and Vestris in their careers. (Head a little this way, if you please, SO; I attend particularly to front faces!) Our profession is ruined by bunglers who understand neither the epoch nor their art. There are dealers in wigs and essences who are enough to make one's hair stand on end; they care only to sell you bottles. It is pitiable! But that's business. Such poor wretches cut hair and dress it as they can. I, when I arrived in Paris from Toulouse, my ambition was to succeed the great Marius, to be a true Marius, to make that name illustrious. I alone, more than all the four others, I said to myself, 'I will conquer, or die.' (There! now sit straight, I am going to finish you.) I was the first to introduce *elegance*; I made my salons the object of curiosity. I disdain advertisements; what advertisements would have cost, monsieur, I put into elegance, charm, comfort. Next year I shall have a quartette in one of the salons to discourse music, and of the best. Yes, we ought to charm away the ennui of those whose heads we dress. I do not conceal from myself the annoyances to a client. (Look at yourself!) To have one's hair dressed is fatiguing, perhaps as much so as posing for one's portrait. Monsieur knows perhaps that the famous Monsieur Humbolt (I did the best I could with the few hairs America left him—science has this in common with savages, that she scalps her men clean), that illustrious savant, said that next to the suffering of going to be hanged was that of going to be painted; but I place the trial of having your head dressed before that of being painted, and so do certain women. Well, monsieur, my object is to make those who come here to have their hair cut or frizzed enjoy themselves. (Hold still, you have a tuft which *must* be conquered.) A Jew proposed to supply me with Italian cantatrices who, during the interludes, were to depilate the young men of forty; but they proved to be girls from the Conservatoire, and music-teachers from the Rue Montmartre. There you are, monsieur; your head is dressed as that of a man of talent ought to be. Ossian," he said to the lacquey in livery, "dress monsieur and show him out. Whose turn next?" he added proudly, gazing round upon the persons who awaited him.

"Don't laugh, Gazonal," said Leon as they reached the foot of the staircase, whence his eye could take in the whole of the Place de la Bourse. "I see over there one of our great men, and you shall compare his language with that of the barber, and tell me which of the two you think the most original."

"Don't laugh, Gazonal," said Bixiou, mimicking Leon's intonation. "What do you suppose is Marius's business?"

"Hair-dressing."

"He has obtained a monopoly of the sale of hair in bulk, as a certain dealer in comestibles who is going to sell us a pate for three francs has acquired a monopoly of the sale of truffles; he discounts the paper of that business; he loans money on pawn to clients when embarrassed; he gives annuities on lives; he gambles at the Bourse; he is a stockholder in all the fashion papers; and he sells, under the name of a certain chemist, an infamous drug which, for his share alone, gives him an income of thirty thousand francs, and costs in advertisements a hundred thousand yearly."

"Is it possible!" cried Gazonal.

"Remember this," said Bixiou, gravely. "In Paris there is no such thing as a small business; all things swell to large proportions, down to the sale of rags and matches. The lemonade-seller who, with his napkin under his arm, meets you as you enter his shop, may be worth his fifty thousand francs a year; the waiter in a restaurant is eligible for the Chamber; the man you take for a beggar in the street carries a hundred thousand francs worth of unset diamonds in his waistcoat pocket, and didn't steal them either."

The three inseparables (for one day at any rate) now crossed the Place de la Bourse in a way to intercept a man about forty years of age, wearing the Legion of honor, who was coming from the boulevard by way of the rue Neuve-Vivienne.

"Hey!" said Leon, "what are you pondering over, my dear Dubourdieu? Some fine symbolic composition? My dear cousin, I have the pleasure to present to you our illustrious painter Dubourdieu, not less celebrated for his humanitarian convictions than for his talents in art. Dubourdieu, my cousin Palafox."

Dubourdieu, a small, pale man with melancholy blue eyes, bowed slightly to Gazonal, who bent low as before a man of genius.

"So you have elected Stidmann in place of—" he began.

"How could I help it? I wasn't there," replied Lora.

"You bring the Academy into disrepute," continued the painter. "To choose such a man as that! I don't wish to say ill of him, but he works at a trade. Where are you dragging the first of arts,—the art those works are the most lasting; bringing nations to light of which the world has long lost even the memory; an art which crowns and consecrates great men? Yes, sculpture is priesthood; it preserves the ideas of an epoch, and you give its chair to a maker of toys and mantelpieces, an ornamentationist, a seller of bric-a-brac! Ah! as Chamfort said, one has to swallow a viper every morning to endure the life of Paris. Well, at any rate, Art remains to a few of us; they can't prevent us from cultivating it—"

"And besides, my dear fellow, you have a consolation which few artists possess; the future is yours," said Bixiou. "When the world is converted to our doctrine, you will be at the head of your art; for you are putting into it ideas which people will understand—*when* they are generalized! In fifty years from now you'll be to all the world what you are to a few of us at this moment,—a great man. The only question is how to get along till then."

"I have just finished," resumed the great artist, his face expanding like that of a man whose hobby is stroked, "an allegorical figure of Harmony; and if you will come and see it, you will understand why it should have taken me two years to paint it. Everything is in it! At the first glance one divines the destiny of the globe. A queen holds a shepherd's crook in her hand,—symbolical of the advancement of the races useful to mankind; she wears on her head the cap of Liberty; her breasts are sixfold, as the Egyptians carved them—for the Egyptians foresaw Fourier; her feet are resting on two clasped hands which embrace a globe,—symbol of the brotherhood of all human races; she tramples cannon under foot to signify the abolition of war; and I have tried to make her face express the serenity of triumphant agriculture. I have also placed beside her an enormous curled cabbage, which, according to our master, is an image of Harmony. Ah! it is not the least among Fourier's titles to veneration that he has restored the gift of thought to plants; he has bound all creation in one by the signification of things to one another, and by their special language. A hundred years hence this earth will be much larger than it is now."

"And how will that, monsieur, come to pass?" said Gazonal, stupefied at hearing a man outside of a lunatic asylum talk in this way.

"Through the extending of production. If men will apply The System, it will not be impossible to act upon the stars."

"What would become of painting in that case?" asked Gazonal.

"It would be magnified."

"Would our eyes be magnified too?" said Gazonal, looking at his two friends significantly.

"Man will return to what he was before he became degenerate; our six-feet men will then be dwarfs."

"Is your picture finished?" asked Leon.

"Entirely finished," replied Dubourdieu. "I have tried to see Hiclar, and get him to compose a symphony for it; I wish that while viewing my picture the public should hear music a la Beethoven to develop its ideas and bring them within range of the intellect by two arts. Ah! if the government would only lend me one of the galleries of the Louvre!"

"I'll mention it, if you want me to do so; you should never neglect an opportunity to strike minds."

"Ah! my friends are preparing articles; but I am afraid they'll go too far."

"Pooh!" said Bixiou, "they can't go as far as the future."

Dubourdieu looked askance at Bixiou, and continued his way.

"Why, he's mad," said Gazonal; "he is following the moon in her courses."

"His skill is masterly," said Leon, "and he knows his art, but Fourierism has killed him. You have just seen, cousin, one of the effects of ambition upon artists. Too often, in Paris, from a desire to reach more rapidly than by natural ways the celebrity which to them is fortune, artists borrow the wings of circumstance, they think they make themselves of more importance as men of a specialty, the supporters of some 'system'; and they fancy they can transform a clique into the public. One is a republican, another Saint-Simonian; this one aristocrat, that one Catholic, others juste-milieu, middle ages, or German, as they choose for their purpose. Now, though opinions do not give talent, they always spoil what talent there is; and the poor fellow whom you have just seen is a proof thereof.

An artist's opinion ought to be: Faith in his art, in his work; and his only way of success is toil when nature has given him the sacred fire."

"Let us get away," said Bixiou. "Leon is beginning to moralize."

"But that man was sincere," said Gazonal, still stupefied.

"Perfectly sincere," replied Bixiou; "as sincere as the king of barbers just now."

"He is mad!" repeated Gazonal.

"And he is not the first man driven man by Fourier's ideas," said Bixiou. "You don't know anything about Paris. Ask it for a hundred thousand francs to realize an idea that will be useful to humanity,—the steam-engine for instance,—and you'll die, like Salomon de Caux, at Bicetre; but if the money is wanted for some paradoxical absurdity, Parisians will annihilate themselves and their fortune for it. It is the same with systems as it is with material things. Utterly impracticable newspapers have consumed millions within the last fifteen years. What makes your lawsuit so hard to win, is that you have right on your side, and on that of the prefect there are (so you suppose) secret motives."

"Do you think that a man of intellect having once understood the nature of Paris could live elsewhere?" said Leon to his cousin.

"Suppose we take Gazonal to old Mere Fontaine?" said Bixiou, making a sign to the driver of a citadine to draw up; "it will be a step from the real to the fantastic. Driver, Vieille rue du Temple."

And all three were presently rolling in the direction of the Marais.

"What are you taking me to see now?" asked Gazonal.

"The proof of what Bixiou told you," replied Leon; "we shall show you a woman who makes twenty thousand francs a year by working a fantastic idea."

"A fortune-teller," said Bixiou, interpreting the look of the Southerner as a question. "Madame Fontaine is thought, by those who seek to pry into the future, to be wiser in her wisdom than Mademoiselle Lenormand."

"She must be very rich," remarked Gazonal.

"She was the victim of her own idea, as long as lotteries existed," said Bixiou; "for in Paris there are no great gains without corresponding outlays. The strongest heads are liable to crack there, as if to give vent to their steam. Those who make much money have vices or fancies,—no doubt to establish an equilibrium."

"And now that the lottery is abolished?" asked Gazonal.

"Oh! now she has a nephew for whom she is hoarding."

When they reached the Vieille rue du Temple the three friends entered one of the oldest houses in that street and passed up a shaking staircase, the steps of which, caked with mud, led them in semi-darkness, and through a stench peculiar to houses on an alley, to the third story, where they beheld a door which painting alone could render; literature would have to spend too many nights in suitably describing it.

An old woman, in keeping with that door, and who might have been that door in human guise, ushered the three friends into a room which served as an ante-chamber, where, in spite of the warm atmosphere which fills the streets of Paris, they felt the icy chill of crypts about them. A damp air came from an inner courtyard which resembled a huge air-shaft; the light that entered was gray, and the sill of the window was filled with pots of sickly plants. In this room, which had a coating of some greasy, fuliginous substance, the furniture, the chairs, the table, were all most abject. The floor tiles oozed like a water-cooler. In short, every accessory was in keeping with the fearful old woman of the hooked nose, ghastly face, and decent rags who directed the "consulters" to sit down, informing them that only one at a time could be admitted to Madame.

Gazonal, who played the intrepid, entered bravely, and found himself in presence of one of those women forgotten by Death, who no doubt forgets them intentionally in order to leave some samples of Itself among the living. He saw before him a withered face in which shone fixed gray eyes of wearying immobility; a flattened nose, smeared with snuff; knuckle-bones well set up by muscles that, under pretence of being hands, played nonchalantly with a pack of cards, like some machine the movement of which is about to run down. The body, a species of broom-handle decently covered with clothes, enjoyed the advantages of death and did not stir. Above the forehead rose a coif of black velvet. Madame Fontaine, for it was really a woman, had a black hen on her right hand and a huge toad, named Astaroth, on her left. Gazonal did not at first perceive them.

The toad, of surprising dimensions, was less alarming in himself than through the effect of two topaz eyes, large as a ten-sous piece, which cast forth vivid gleams. It was impossible to endure that look. The toad is a creature as yet unexplained. Perhaps the whole animal creation, including man, is comprised in it; for, as Lassailly said, the toad exists indefinitely; and, as we know, it is of all created animals the one whose marriage lasts the longest.

The black hen had a cage about two feet distant from the table, covered with a green cloth, to which she came along a plank which formed a sort of drawbridge between the cage and the table.

When the woman, the least real of the creatures in this Hoffmanesque den, said to Gazonal: "Cut!" the worthy provincial shuddered involuntarily. That which renders these beings so formidable is the importance of what we want to know. People go to them, as they know very well, to buy hope.

The den of the sibyl was much darker than the antechamber; the color of the walls could scarcely be distinguished. The ceiling, blackened by smoke, far from reflecting the little light that came from a window obstructed by pale and sickly vegetations, absorbed the greater part of it; but the table where the sorceress sat received what there was of this half-light fully. The table, the chair of the woman, and that on which Gazonal was seated, formed the entire furniture of the little room, which was divided at one end by a sort of loft where Madame Fontaine probably slept. Gazonal heard through a half-opened door the bubbling murmur of a soup-pot. That kitchen sound, accompanied by a composite odor in which the effluvia of a sink predominated, mingled incongruous ideas of the necessities of actual life with those of supernatural power. Disgust entered into curiosity.

Gazonal observed one stair of pine wood, the lowest no doubt of the staircase which led to the loft. He took in these minor details at a glance, with a sense of nausea. It was all quite otherwise alarming than the romantic tales and scenes of German drama lead one to expect; here was suffocating actuality. The air diffused a sort of dizzy heaviness, the dim light rasped the nerves. When the Southerner, impelled by a species of self-assertion, gazed firmly at the toad, he felt a sort of emetic heat at the pit of his stomach, and was conscious of a terror like that a criminal might feel in presence of a gendarme. He endeavoured to brace himself by looking at Madame Fontaine; but there he encountered two almost white eyes, the motionless and icy pupils of which were absolutely intolerable to him. The silence became terrifying.

"Which do you wish, monsieur, the five-franc fortune, the ten-franc fortune, or the grand game?"

"The five-franc fortune is dear enough," replied the Southerner, making powerful efforts not to yield to the influence of the surroundings in which he found himself.

At the moment when Gazonal was thus endeavouring to collect himself, a voice—an infernal voice—made him bound in his chair; the black hen clucked.

"Go back, my daughter, go back; monsieur chooses to spend only five francs."

The hen seemed to understand her mistress, for, after coming within a foot of the cards, she turned and resumed her former place.

"What flower to you like best?" asked the old woman, in a voice hoarsened by the phlegm which seemed to rise and fall incessantly in her bronchial tubes.

"The rose."

"What color are you fond of?"

"Blue."

"What animal do you prefer?"

"The horse. Why these questions?" he asked.

"Man derives his form from his anterior states," she said sententiously. "Hence his instincts; and his instincts rule his destiny. What food do you like best to eat,—fish, game, cereals, butcher's meat, sweet things, vegetables, or fruits?"

"Game."

"In what month where you born?"

"September."

"Put out your hand."

Madame Fontaine looked attentively at the lines of the hand that was shown to her. It was all done seriously, with no pretence of sorcery; on the contrary, with the simplicity a notary might have shown when asking the intentions of a client about a deed. Presently she shuffled the cards, and asked Gazonal to cut them, and then to make three packs of them himself. After which she took the packs, spread them out before her, and examined them as a gambler examines the thirty-six numbers at roulette before he risks his stake. Gazonal's bones were freezing; he seemed not to know where he was; but his amazement grew greater and greater when this hideous old woman in a green bonnet, stout and squat, whose false front was frizzed into points of interrogation, proceeded, in a thick voice, to relate to him all the particular circumstances, even the most secret, of his past life: she told him his tastes, his habits, his character; the thoughts of his childhood; everything that had influenced his life; a marriage broken off, why, with whom, the exact description of the woman he had loved; and, finally, the place he came from, his lawsuit, etc.

Gazonal at first thought it was a hoax prepared by his companions; but the absolute impossibility of such a conspiracy appeared to him almost as soon as the idea itself, and he sat speechless before that truly infernal power, the incarnation of which borrowed from humanity a form which the imagination of painters and poets has throughout all ages regarded as the most awful of created things,—namely, a toothless, hideous, wheezing hag, with cold lips, flattened nose, and whitish eyes. The pupils of those eyes had brightened, through them rushed a ray,—was it from the depths of the future or from hell?

Gazonal asked, interrupting the old creature, of what use the toad and the hen were to her.

"They predict the future. The consulter himself throws grain upon the cards; Bilouche comes and pecks it. Astaroth crawls over the cards to get the food the client holds for him, and those two wonderful intelligences are never mistaken. Will you see them at work?—you will then know your future. The cost is a hundred francs."

Gazonal, horrified by the gaze of Astaroth, rushed into the antechamber, after bowing to the terrible old woman. He was moist from head to foot, as if under the incubation of some evil spirit.

"Let us get away!" he said to the two artists. "Did you ever consult that sorceress?"

"I never do anything important without getting Astaroth's opinion," said Leon, "and I am always the better for it."

"I'm expecting the virtuous fortune which Bilouche has promised me," said Bixiou.

"I've a fever," cried Gazonal. "If I believed what you say I should have to believe in sorcery, in some supernatural power."

"It may be only natural," said Bixiou. "One-third of all the lorettes, one-fourth of all the statesmen, and one-half of all artists consult Madame Fontaine; and I know a minister to whom she is an Egeria."

"Did she tell you about your future?" asked Leon.

"No; I had enough of her about my past. But," added Gazonal, struck by a sudden thought, "if she can, by the help of those dreadful collaborators, predict the future, how came she to lose in the lottery?"

"Ah! you put your finger on one of the greatest mysteries of occult science," replied Leon. "The moment that the species of inward mirror on which the past or the future is reflected to their minds become clouded by the breath of a personal feeling, by an idea foreign to the purpose of the power they are exerting, sorcerers and sorceresses can see nothing; just as an artist who blurs art with political combinations and systems loses his genius. Not long ago, a man endowed with the gift of divining by cards, a rival to Madame Fontaine, became addicted to vicious practices, and being unable to tell his own fate from the cards, was arrested, tried, and condemned at the court of assizes. Madame Fontaine, who predicts the future eight times out of ten, was never able to know if she would win or lose in a lottery."

"It is the same thing in magnetism," remarked Bixiou. "A man can't magnetize himself."

"Heavens! now we come to magnetism!" cried Gazonal. "Ah ca! do you know everything?"

"Friend Gazonal," replied Bixiou, gravely, "to be able to laugh at everything one must know everything. As for me, I've been in Paris since my childhood; I've lived, by means of my pencil, on its follies and absurdities, at the rate of five caricatures a month. Consequently, I often laugh at ideas in which I have faith."

"Come, let us get to something else," said Leon. "We'll go to the Chamber and settle the cousin's affair."

"This," said Bixiou, imitating Odry in "Les Funambules," "is high comedy, for we will make the first orator we meet pose for us, and you shall see that in those halls of legislation, as elsewhere, the Parisian language has but two tones,—Self-interest, Vanity."

As they got into their citadine, Leon saw in a rapidly driven cabriolet a man to whom he made a sign that he had something to say to him.

"There's Publicola Masson," said Leon to Bixiou. "I'm going to ask for a sitting this evening at five o'clock, after the Chamber. The cousin shall then see the most curious of all the originals."

"Who is he?" asked Gazonal, while Leon went to speak to Publicola Masson.

"An artist-pedicure," replied Bixiou, "author of a 'Treatise on Corporistics,' who cuts your corns by subscription, and who, if the Republications triumph for six months, will assuredly become immortal."

"Drives his carriage!" ejaculated Gazonal.

"But, my good Gazonal, it is only millionaires who have time to go afoot in Paris."

"To the Chamber!" cried Leon to the coachman, getting back into the carriage.

"Which, monsieur?"

"Deputies," replied Leon, exchanging a smile with Bixiou.

"Paris begins to confound me," said Gazonal.

"To make you see its immensity,—moral, political, and literary,—we are now proceeding like the Roman cicerone, who shows you in Saint Peter's the thumb of the statue you took to be life-size, and the thumb proves to be a foot long. You haven't yet measured so much as a great toe of Paris."

"And remark, cousin Gazonal, that we take things as they come; we haven't selected."

"This evening you shall sup as they feasted at Belshazzar's; and there you shall see our Paris, our own particular Paris, playing lansquenet, and risking a hundred thousand francs at a throw without winking."

A quarter of an hour later the citadine stopped at the foot of the steps going up to the Chamber of Deputies, at that end of the Pont de la Concorde which leads to discord.

"I thought the Chamber unapproachable?" said the provincial, surprised to find himself in the great lobby.

"That depends," replied Bixiou; "materially speaking, it costs thirty sous for a citadine to approach it; politically, you have to spend rather more. The swallows thought, so a poet says, that the Arc de Triomphe was erected for them; we artists think that this public building was built for us,—to compensate for the stupidities of the Theatre-Francais and make us laugh; but the comedians on this stage are much more expensive; and they don't give us every day the value of our money."

"So this is the Chamber!" cried Gazonal, as he paced the great hall in which there were then about a dozen persons, and looked around him with an air which Bixiou noted down in his memory and reproduced in one of the famous caricatures with which he rivalled Gavarni.

Leon went to speak to one of the ushers who go and come continually between this hall and the hall of sessions, with which it communicates by a passage in which are stationed the stenographers of the "Moniteur" and persons attached to the Chamber.

"As for the minister," replied the usher to Leon as Gazonal approached them, "he is there, but I don't know if Monsieur Giraud has come. I'll see."

As the usher opened one side of the double door through which none but deputies, ministers, or messengers from the king are allowed to pass, Gazonal saw a man come out who seemed still young, although he was really forty-eight years old, and to whom the usher evidently indicated Leon de Lora.

"Ha! you here!" he exclaimed, shaking hands with both Bixiou and Lora. "Scamps! what are you doing in the sanctuary of the laws?"

"Parbleu! we've come to learn how to blague," said Bixiou. "We might get rusty if we didn't."

"Let us go into the garden," said the young man, not observing that Gazonal belonged to the party.

Seeing that this new-comer was well-dressed, in black, the provincial did not know in which political category to place him; but he followed the others into the garden contiguous to the hall which follows the line of the quai Napoleon. Once in the garden the ci-devant young man gave way to a peal of laughter which he seemed to have been repressing since he entered the lobby.

"What is it?" asked Leon de Lora.

"My dear friend, to prove the sincerity of the constitutional government we are forced to tell the most frightful lies with incredible self-possession. But as for me, I'm freakish; some days I can lie like a prospectus; other days I can't be serious. This is one of my hilarious days. Now, at this moment, the prime minister, being summoned by the Opposition to make known a certain diplomatic secret, is going through his paces in the tribune. Being an honest man who never lies on his own account, he whispered to me as he mounted the breach: 'Heaven knows what I shall say to them.' A mad desire to laugh overcame me, and as one mustn't laugh on the ministerial bench I rushed out, for my youth does come back to me most unseasonably at times."

"At last," cried Gazonal, "I've found an honest man in Paris! You must be a very superior man," he added, looking at the stranger.

"Ah ca! who is this gentleman?" said the ci-devant young man, examining Gazonal.

"My cousin," said Leon, hastily. "I'll answer for his silence and his honor as for my own. It is on his account we have come here now; he has a case before the administration which depends on your ministry. His prefect evidently wants to ruin him, and we have come to see you in order to prevent the Council of State from ratifying a great injustice."

"Who brings up the case?"

"Massol."

"Good."

"And our friends Giraud and Claude Vignon are on the committee," said Bixiou.

"Say just a word to them," urged Leon; "tell them to come to-night to Carabine's, where du Tillet gives a fete apropos of railways,—they are plundering more than ever on the roads."

"Ah ca! but isn't your cousin from the Pyrenees?" asked the young man, now become serious.

"Yes," replied Gazonal.

"And you did not vote for us in the last elections?" said the statesman, looking hard at Gazonal.

"No; but what you have just said in my hearing has bribed me; on the word of a commandant of the National Guard I'll have your candidate elected—"

"Very good; will you guarantee your cousin?" asked the young man, turning to Leon.

"We are forming him," said Bixiou, in a tone irresistibly comic.

"Well, I'll see about it," said the young man, leaving his friends and rushing precipitately back to the Chamber.

"Who is that?" asked Gazonal.

"The Comte de Rastignac; the minister of the department in which your affair is brought up."

"A minister! Isn't a minister anything more than that?"

"He is an old friend of ours. He now has three hundred thousand francs a year; he's a peer of France; the king has made him a count; he married Nucingen's daughter; and he is one of the two or three statesmen produced by the revolution of July. But his fame and his power bore him sometimes, and he comes down to laugh with us."

"Ah ça! cousin; why didn't you tell us you belonged to the Opposition?" asked Leon, seizing Gazonal by the arm. "How stupid of you! One deputy more or less to Right or Left and your bed is made."

"We are all for the Others down my way."

"Let 'em go," said Bixiou, with a facetious look; "they have Providence on their side, and Providence will bring them back without you and in spite of themselves. A manufacturer ought to be a fatalist."

"What luck! There's Maxime, with Canalis and Giraud," said Leon.

"Come along, friend Gazonal, the promised actors are mustering on the stage," said Bixiou.

And all three advanced to the above-named personages, who seemed to be sauntering along with nothing to do.

"Have they turned you out, or why are you idling about in this way?" said Bixiou to Giraud.

"No, while they are voting by secret ballot we have come out for a little air," replied Giraud.

"How did the prime minister pull through?"

"He was magnificent!" said Canalis.

"Magnificent!" repeated Maxime.

"Magnificent!" cried Giraud.

"So! so! Right, Left, and Centre are unanimous!"

"All with a different meaning," observed Maxime de Trailles.

Maxime was the ministerial deputy.

"Yes," said Canalis, laughing.

Though Canalis had already been a minister, he was at this moment tending toward the Right.

"Ah! but you had a fine triumph just now," said Maxime to Canalis; "it was you who forced the minister into the tribune."

"And made him lie like a charlatan," returned Canalis.

"A worthy victory," said the honest Giraud. "In his place what would you have done?"

"I should have lied."

"It isn't called lying," said Maxime de Trailles; "it is called protecting the crown."

So saying, he led Canalis away to a little distance.

"That's a great orator," said Leon to Giraud, pointing to Canalis.

"Yes and no," replied the councillor of state. "A fine bass voice, and sonorous, but more of an artist in words than an orator. In short, he's a fine instrument but he isn't music, consequently he has not, and he never will have, the ear of the Chamber; in no case will he ever be master of the situation."

Canalis and Maxime were returning toward the little group as Giraud, deputy of the Left Centre, pronounced this verdict. Maxime took Giraud by the arm and led him off, probably to make the same confidence he had just made Canalis.

"What an honest, upright fellow that is," said Leon to Canalis, nodding towards Giraud.

"One of those upright fellows who kill administrators," replied Canalis.

"Do you think him a good orator?"

"Yes and no," replied Canalis; "he is wordy; he's long-winded, a plodder in argument, and a good logician; but he doesn't understand the higher logic, that of events and circumstances; consequently he has never had, and never will have, the ear of the Chamber."

At the moment when Canalis uttered this judgment on Giraud, the latter was returning with Maxime to the group; and forgetting the presence of a stranger whose discretion was not known to them like that of Leon and Bixiou, he took Canalis by the hand in a very significant manner.

"Well," he said, "I consent to what Monsieur de Trailles proposes. I'll put the question to you in the Chamber, but I shall do it with great severity."

"Then we shall have the house with us, for a man of your weight and your eloquence is certain to have the ear of the Chamber," said Canalis. "I'll reply to you; but I shall do it sharply, to crush you."

"You could bring about a change of the cabinet, for on such ground you can do what you like with the Chamber, and be master of the situation."

"Maxime has trapped them both," said Leon to his cousin; "that fellow is like a fish in water among the intrigues of the Chamber."

"Who is he?" asked Gazonal.

"An ex-scoundrel who is now in a fair way to become an ambassador," replied Bixiou.

"Giraud!" said Leon to the councillor of state, "don't leave the Chamber without asking Rastignac what he promised to tell you about a suit you are to render a decision on two days hence. It concerns my cousin here; I'll go and see you to-morrow morning early about it."

The three friends followed the three deputies, at a distance, into the lobby.

"Cousin, look at those two men," said Leon, pointing out to him a former minister and the leader of the Left Centre. "Those are two men who really have 'the ear of the Chamber,' and who are called in jest ministers of the department of the Opposition. They have the ear of the Chamber so completely that they are always pulling it."

"It is four o'clock," said Bixiou, "let us go back to the rue de Berlin."

"Yes; you've now seen the heart of the government, cousin, and you must next be shown the ascarides, the taenia, the intestinal worm,—the republican, since I must needs name him," said Leon.

When the three friends were once more packed into their hackney-coach, Gazonal looked at his cousin and Bixiou like a man who had a mind to launch a flood of oratorical and Southern bile upon the elements.

"I distrusted with all my might this great hussy of a town," he rolled out in Southern accents; "but since this morning I despise her! The poor little province you think so petty is an honest girl; but Paris is a prostitute, a greedy, lying comedian; and I am very thankful not to be robbed of my skin in it."

"The day is not over yet," said Bixiou, sententiously, winking at Leon.

"And why do you complain in that stupid way," said Leon, "of a prostitution to which you will owe the winning of your lawsuit? Do you think you are more virtuous than we, less of a comedian, less greedy, less liable to fall under some temptation, less conceited than those we have been making dance for you like puppets?"

"Try me!"

"Poor lad!" said Leon, shrugging his shoulders, "haven't you already promised Rastignac your electoral influence?"

"Yes, because he was the only one who ridiculed himself."

"Poor lad!" repeated Bixiou, "why slight me, who am always ridiculing myself? You are like a pug-dog barking at a tiger. Ha! if you saw us really ridiculing a man, you'd see that we can drive a sane man mad."

This conversation brought Gazonal back to his cousin's house, where the sight of luxury silenced him, and put an end to the discussion. Too late he perceived that Bixiou had been making him pose.

At half-past five o'clock, the moment when Leon de Lora was making his evening toilet to the great wonderment of Gazonal, who counted the thousand and one superfluities of his cousin, and admired the solemnity of the valet as he performed his functions, the "pedicure of monsieur" was announced, and Publicola Masson, a little man fifty years of age, made his appearance, laid a small box of instruments on the floor, and sat down on a small chair opposite to Leon, after bowing to Gazonal and Bixiou.

"How are matters going with you?" asked Leon, delivering to Publicola one of his feet, already washed and prepared by the valet.

"I am forced to take two pupils,—two young fellows who, despairing of fortune, have quitted surgery for corporistics; they were actually dying of hunger; and yet they are full of talent."

"I'm not asking you about pedestrial affairs, I want to know how you are getting on politically."

Masson gave a glance at Gazonal, more eloquent than any species of question.

"Oh! you can speak out, that's my cousin; in a way he belongs to you; he thinks himself legitimist."

"Well! we are coming along, we are advancing! In five years from now Europe will be with us. Switzerland and Italy are fermenting finely; and when the occasion comes we are all ready. Here, in Paris, we have fifty thousand armed men, without counting two hundred thousand citizens who haven't a penny to live upon."

"Pooh," said Leon, "how about the fortifications?"

"Pie-crust; we can swallow them," replied Masson.

"In the first place, we sha'n't let the cannon in, and, in the second, we've got a little machine more powerful than all the forts in the world,—a machine, due to a doctor, which cured more people during the short time we worked it than the doctors ever killed."

"How you talk!" exclaimed Gazonal, whose flesh began to creep at Publicola's air and manner.

"Ha! that's the thing we rely on! We follow Saint-Just and Robespierre; but we'll do better than they; they were timid, and you see what came of it; an emperor! the elder branch! the younger branch! The Montagnards didn't lop the social tree enough."

"Ah ca! you, who will be, they tell me, consul, or something of that kind, tribune perhaps, be good enough to remember," said Bixiou, "that I have asked your protection for the last dozen years."

"No harm shall happen to you; we shall need wags, and you can take the place of Barere," replied the corn-doctor.

"And I?" said Leon.

"Ah, you! you are my client, and that will save you; for genius is an odious privilege, to which too much is accorded in France; we shall be forced to annihilate some of our greatest men in order to teach others to be simple citizens."

The corn-cutter spoke with a semi-serious, semi-jesting air that made Gazonal shudder.

"So," he said, "there's to be no more religion?"

"No more religion *of the State*," replied the pedicure, emphasizing the last words; "every man will have his own. It is very fortunate that the government is just now endowing convents; they'll provide our funds. Everything, you see, conspires in our favour. Those who pity the peoples, who clamor on behalf of proletaries, who write works against the Jesuits, who busy themselves about the amelioration of no matter what,—the communists, the humanitarians, the philanthropists, you understand,—all these people are our advanced guard. While we are storing gunpowder, they are making the tinder which the spark of a single circumstance will ignite."

"But what do you expect will make the happiness of France?" cried Gazonal.

"Equality of citizens and cheapness of provisions. We mean that there will be no persons lacking anything, no millionaires, no suckers of blood and victims."

"That's it!—maximum and minimum," said Gazonal.

"You've said it," replied the corn-cutter, decisively.

"No more manufacturers?" asked Gazonal.

"The state will manufacture. We shall all be the usufructuaries of France; each will have his ration as on board ship; and all the world will work according to their capacity."

"Ah!" said Gazonal, "and while awaiting the time when you can cut off the heads of aristocrats—"

"I cut their nails," said the radical republican, putting up his tools and finishing the jest himself.

Then he bowed very politely and went away.

"Can this be possible in 1845?" cried Gazonal.

"If there were time we could show you," said his cousin, "all the personages of 1793, and you could talk with them. You have just seen Marat; well! we know Fouquier-Tinville, Collot d'Herbois, Robespierre, Chabot, Fouche, Barras; there is even a magnificent Madame Roland."

"Well, the tragic is not lacking in your play," said Gazonal.

"It is six o'clock. Before we take you to see Odry in 'Les Saltimbauques' to-night," said Leon to Gazonal, "we must go and pay a visit to Madame Cadine,—an actress whom your committee-man Massol cultivates, and to whom you must therefore pay the most assiduous court."

"And as it is all important that you conciliate that power, I am going to give you a few instructions," said Bixiou. "Do you employ workwomen in your manufactory?"

"Of course I do," replied Gazonal.

"That's all I want to know," resumed Bixiou. "You are not married, and you are a great—"

"Yes!" cried Gazonal, "you've guessed my strong point, I'm a great lover of women."

"Well, then! if you will execute the little manoeuvre which I am about to prescribe for you, you will taste, without spending a farthing, the sweets to be found in the good graces of an actress."

When they reached the rue de la Victoire where the celebrated actress lived, Bixiou, who meditated a trick upon the distrustful provincial, had scarcely finished teaching him his role; but Gazonal was quick, as we shall see, to take a hint.

The three friends went up to the second floor of a rather handsome house, and found Madame Jenny Cadine just finishing dinner, for she played that night in an afterpiece at the Gymnase. Having presented Gazonal to this great power, Leon and Bixiou, in order to leave them alone together, made the excuse of looking at a piece of furniture in another room; but before leaving, Bixiou had whispered in the actress's ear: "He is Leon's cousin, a manufacturer, enormously rich; he wants to win a suit before the Council of State against his prefect, and he thinks it wise to fascinate you in order to get Massol on his side."

All Paris knows the beauty of that young actress, and will therefore understand the stupefaction of the Southerner on seeing her. Though she had received him at first rather coldly, he became the object of her good graces before they had been many minutes alone together.

"How strange!" said Gazonal, looking round him disdainfully on the furniture of the salon, the door of which his accomplices had left half open, "that a woman like you should be allowed to live in such an ill-furnished apartment."

"Ah, yes, indeed! but how can I help it? Massol is not rich; I am hoping he will be made a minister."

"What a happy man!" cried Gazonal, heaving the sigh of a provincial.

"Good!" thought she. "I shall have new furniture, and get the better of Carabine."

"Well, my dear!" said Leon, returning, "you'll be sure to come to Carabine's to-night, won't you?—supper and lansquenet."

"Will monsieur be there?" said Jenny Cadine, looking artlessly and graciously at Gazonal.

"Yes, madame," replied the countryman, dazzled by such rapid success.

"But Massol will be there," said Bixiou.

"Well, what of that?" returned Jenny. "Come, we must part, my treasures; I must go to the theatre."

Gazonal gave his hand to the actress, and led her to the citadine which was waiting for her; as he did so he pressed hers with such ardor that Jenny Cadine exclaimed, shaking her fingers: "Take care! I haven't any others."

When the three friends got back into their own vehicle, Gazonal endeavoured to seize Bixiou round the waist, crying out: "She bites! You're a fine rascal!"

"So women say," replied Bixiou.

At half-past eleven o'clock, after the play, another citadine took the trio to the house of Mademoiselle Seraphine Sinet, better known under the name of Carabine,—one of those pseudonyms which famous lorettes take, or which are given to them; a name which, in this instance, may have referred to the pigeons she had killed.

Carabine, now become almost a necessity for the banker du Tillet, deputy of the Left, lived in a charming house in the rue Saint-Georges. In Paris there are many houses the destination of which never varies; and the one we now speak of had already seen seven careers of courtesans. A broker had brought there, about the year 1827, Suzanne du Val-Noble, afterwards Madame Gaillard. In that house the famous Esther caused the Baron de Nucingen to commit the only follies of his life. Florine, and subsequently, a person now called in jest "the late Madame Schontz," had scintillated there in turn. Bored by his wife, du Tillet bought this modern little house, and there installed the celebrated Carabine, whose lively wit and cavalier manners and shameless brilliancy were a counterpoise to the dulness of domestic life, and the toils of finance and politics.

Whether du Tillet or Carabine were at home or not at home, supper was served, and splendidly served, for ten persons every day. Artists, men of letters, journalists, and the habitues of the house supped there when they pleased. After supper they gambled. More than one member of both Chambers came there to buy what Paris pays for by its weight in gold,—namely, the amusement of intercourse with anomalous untrammelled women, those meteors of the Parisian firmament who are so difficult to class. There wit reigns; for all can be said, and all is said. Carabine, a rival of the no less celebrated Malaga, had finally inherited the salon of Florine, now Madame Raoul Nathan, and of Madame Schontz, now wife of Chief-Justice du Ronceret.

As he entered, Gazonal made one remark only, but that remark was both legitimate and legitimist: "It is finer than the Tuileries!" The satins, velvets, brocades, the gold, the objects of art that swarmed there, so filled the eyes of the wary provincial that at first he did not see Madame Jenny Cadine, in a toilet intended to inspire respect, who, concealed behind Carabine, watched his entrance observingly, while conversing with others.

"My dear child," said Leon to Carabine, "this is my cousin, a manufacturer, who descended upon me from the Pyrenees this morning. He knows nothing of Paris, and he wants Massol to help him in a suit he has before the Council of State. We have therefore taken the liberty to bring him—his name is Gazonal—to supper, entreating you to leave him his full senses."

"That's as monsieur pleases; wine is dear," said Carabine, looking Gazonal over from head to foot, and thinking him in no way remarkable.

Gazonal, bewildered by the toilets, the lights, the gilding, the chatter of the various groups whom he thought to be discussing him, could only manage to stammer out the words: "Madame—madame—is—very good."

"What do you manufacture?" said the mistress of the house, laughing.

"Say laces and offer her some guipure," whispered Bixiou in Gazonal's ear.

"La-ces," said Gazonal, perceiving that he would have to pay for his supper. "It will give me the greatest pleasure to offer you a dress—a scarf—a mantilla of my make."

"Ah, three things! Well, you are nicer than you look to be," returned Carabine.

"Paris has caught me!" thought Gazonal, now perceiving Jenny Cadine, and going up to her.

"And I," said the actress, "what am I to have?"

"All I possess," replied Gazonal, thinking that to offer all was to give nothing.

Massol, Claude Vignon, du Tillet, Maxime de Trailles, Nucingen, du Bruel, Malaga, Monsieur and Madame Gaillard, Vauvinet, and a crowd of other personages now entered.

After a conversation with the manufacturer on the subject of his suit, Massol, without making any promises, told him that the report was not yet written, and that citizens could always rely on the knowledge and the independence of the Council of State. Receiving that cold and dignified response, Gazonal, in despair, thought it necessary to set about seducing the charming Jenny, with whom he was by this time in love. Leon de Lora and Bixiou left their victim in the hands of that most roguish and frolicsome member of the anomalous society,—for Jenny Cadine is the sole rival in that respect of the famous Dejazet.

At the supper-table, where Gazonal was fascinated by a silver service made by the modern Benvenuto Cellini, Froment-Meurice, the contents of which were worthy of the container, his mischievous friends were careful to sit at some distance from him; but they followed with cautious eye the manoeuvres of the clever actress, who, being attracted by the insidious hope of getting her furniture renewed, was playing her cards to take the provincial home with her.

No sheep upon the day of the Fete-Dieu ever more meekly allowed his little Saint John to lead him along than Gazonal as he followed his siren.

Three days later, Leon and Bixiou, who had not seen Gazonal since that evening, went to his lodgings about two in the afternoon.

"Well, cousin," said Leon, "the Council of State has decided in favour of your suit."

"Maybe, but it is useless now, cousin," said Gazonal, lifting a melancholy eye to his two friends. "I've become a republican."

"What does that mean?" asked Leon.

"I haven't anything left; not even enough to pay my lawyer," replied Gazonal. "Madame Jenny Cadine has got notes of hand out of me to the amount of more money than all the property I own—"

"The fact is Cadine is rather dear; but—"

"Oh, but I didn't get anything for my money," said Gazonal. "What a woman! Well, I'll own the provinces are not a match for Paris; I shall retire to La Trappe."

"Good!" said Bixiou, "now you are reasonable. Come, recognize the majesty of the capital."

"And of capital," added Leon, holding out to Gazonal his notes of hand.

Gazonal gazed at the papers with a stupefied air.

"You can't say now that we don't understand the duties of hospitality; haven't we educated you, saved you from poverty, feasted you, and amused you?" said Bixiou.

"*And* fooled you," added Leon, making the gesture of gamins to express the action of picking pockets.

ADDENDUM

The following personages appear in other stories of the Human Comedy.

Brambourg, Comte de
   A Bachelor's Establishment

Cadine, Jenny
   Cousin Betty
   Beatrix
   The Member for Arcis

Canalis, Constant-Cyr-Melchior, Baron de
   Letters of Two Brides
   A Distinguished Provincial at Paris
   Modeste Mignon
   The Magic Skin
   Another Study of Woman
   A Start in Life
   Beatrix
   The Member for Arcis

Collin, Jacqueline
   Scenes from a Courtesan's Life
   Cousin Betty

Fontaine, Madame
   Cousin Pons

Gaillard, Theodore
   A Distinguished Provincial at Paris
   Beatrix
   Scenes from a Courtesan's Life

Gaillard, Madame Theodore
   Jealousies of a Country Town
   A Distinguished Provincial at Paris
   A Bachelor's Establishment
   Scenes from a Courtesan's Life
   Beatrix

Giraud, Leon
   A Distinguished Provincial at Paris
   A Bachelor's Establishment
   The Secrets of a Princess

Gobseck, Jean-Esther Van
   Gobseck
   Father Goriot
   Cesar Birotteau
   The Government Clerks

Lora, Leon de
   A Bachelor's Establishment
   A Start in Life
   Pierre Grassou
   Honorine
   Cousin Betty
   Beatrix

Lousteau, Etienne
   A Distinguished Provincial at Paris
   A Bachelor's Establishment
   Scenes from a Courtesan's Life

A Daughter of Eve
  Beatrix
  The Muse of the Department
  Cousin Betty
  A Prince of Bohemia
  A Man of Business
  The Middle Classes

Marsay, Henri de
  The Thirteen
  Another Study of Woman
  The Lily of the Valley
  Father Goriot
  Jealousies of a Country Town
  Ursule Mirouet
  A Marriage Settlement
  Lost Illusions
  A Distinguished Provincial at Paris
  Letters of Two Brides
  The Ball at Sceaux
  Modest Mignon
  The Secrets of a Princess
  The Gondreville Mystery
  A Daughter of Eve

Massol
  Scenes from a Courtesan's Life
  The Magic Skin
  A Daughter of Eve
  Cousin Betty

Nathan, Raoul
  Lost Illusions
  A Distinguished Provincial at Paris
  Scenes from a Courtesan's Life

    The Secrets of a Princess
    A Daughter of Eve
    Letters of Two Brides
    The Seamy Side of History
    The Muse of the Department
    A Prince of Bohemia
    A Man of Business

Nathan, Madame Raoul
    The Muse of the Department
    Lost Illusions
    A Distinguished Provincial at Paris
    Scenes from a Courtesan's Life
    The Government Clerks
    A Bachelor's Establishment
    Ursule Mirouet
    Eugenie Grandet
    The Imaginary Mistress
    A Prince of Bohemia
    A Daughter of Eve

Nourrisson, Madame
    Scenes from a Courtesan's Life
    Cousin Betty

Nucingen, Baron Frederic de
    The Firm of Nucingen
    Father Goriot
    Pierrette
    Cesar Birotteau
    Lost Illusions
    A Distinguished Provincial at Paris
    Scenes from a Courtesan's Life
    Another Study of Woman
    The Secrets of a Princess

    A Man of Business
    Cousin Betty
    The Muse of the Department

Rastignac, Eugene de
    Father Goriot
    A Distinguished Provincial at Paris
    Scenes from a Courtesan's Life
    The Ball at Sceaux
    The Interdiction
    A Study of Woman
    Another Study of Woman
    The Magic Skin
    The Secrets of a Princess
    A Daughter of Eve
    The Gondreville Mystery
    The Firm of Nucingen
    Cousin Betty
    The Member for Arcis

Ridal, Fulgence
    A Bachelor's Establishment
    A Distinguished Provincial at Paris

Ronceret, Madame Fabien du
    Beatrix
    The Muse of the Department
    Cousin Betty

Schinner, Hippolyte
    The Purse
    A Bachelor's Establishment
    Pierre Grassou
    A Start in Life
    Albert Savarus

    The Government Clerks
    Modeste Mignon
    The Imaginary Mistress

Sinet, Seraphine
    Cousin Betty

Stidmann
    Modeste Mignon
    Beatrix
    The Member for Arcis
    Cousin Betty
    Cousin Pons

Tillet, Ferdinand du
    Cesar Birotteau
    The Firm of Nucingen
    The Middle Classes
    A Bachelor's Establishment
    Pierrette
    Melmoth Reconciled
    A Distinguished Provincial at Paris
    The Secrets of a Princess
    A Daughter of Eve
    The Member for Arcis
    Cousin Betty

Trailles, Comte Maxime de
    Cesar Birotteau
    Father Goriot
    Gobseck
    Ursule Mirouet
    A Man of Business
    The Member for Arcis
    The Secrets of a Princess

Cousin Betty
The Member for Arcis
Beatrix

Vauvinet
  Cousin Betty

Vignon, Claude
  A Distinguished Provincial at Paris
  A Daughter of Eve
  Honorine
  Beatrix
  Cousin Betty

BIBLIOBAZAAR

The essential book market!

Did you know that you can get any of our titles in large print?

Did you know that we have an ever-growing collection of books in many languages?

Order online:
www.bibliobazaar.com

Find all of your favorite classic books!

Stay up to date with the latest government reports!

At BiblioBazaar, we aim to make knowledge more accessible by making thousands of titles available to you- *quickly and affordably*.

Contact us:
BiblioBazaar
PO Box 21206
Charleston, SC 29413